# Riding the Dog

nine bus stories

by

## Sybil Rosen

March 2016

For Fred and Mary,

And the buddha in the seat
next to you.

Love,

Sybil Rosen

Publisher: BookBaby www.BookBaby.com

Publication Date: December 2014

ISBN: 978-1-63192-508-5

Book Design: BookBaby

For Glyn

# Table of Contents

I'm going down to the Greyhound station
Gonna get a ticket to ride
Gonna find that lady with two or three kids
And sit down by her side

> *Blaze Foley, "Clay Pigeons"*


She never thought this would be the place
Where she would find her saving grace
But she fell in love, she fell in love
On the backseat of a Greyhound bus

> *Sara Evans, "Backseat of a Greyhound Bus"*


You may bury my body, ooh, down by the highway side
So my old evil spirit can catch a Greyhound bus and ride

> *Robert Johnson, "Me And The Devil"*

# Change in Kingston

The driver knew her by her perfume. She had been a regular on his route for months. Every other Tuesday afternoon he had come to expect her. Gilbert Craddock was a large-limbed African-American in his early fifties, though he showed few signs of wear. A veteran of the Gulf War, Gil prided himself on his professionalism. The creases in his uniform trousers were as crisp and ironclad as his self-imposed rule: never get involved with a passenger.

The scent of crushed orchids announced the woman's arrival. Gil did not know a crushed orchid from an uncrushed one, but those were the words her perfume brought to mind. He took her ticket, careful not to make eye contact. She was tall and young and clad from head to toe in hooded robes. This afternoon her downturned face was framed in fabric neither blue nor gray but a shade in-between, the color of fog. The *chador*'s hood fell in a straight line above dark eyebrows curving thickly over blue-green eyes shot with amber. She might have been Persian, or one of those Eastern European Muslims, Gil could not tell. It was a harmless game he liked to play, speculating on the bloodlines of his more exotic passengers.

He had seen many women clothed like her during his service in Kuwait. Her appearance was always a jolt in time, but this was more than that. Names had been required on tickets since the 9/11 terrorist attack, but hers – D. LaSalle – gave no real clue to her origins. The voluminous cloak made it impossible for him to guess her shape, though that had not kept him from trying. He had not even realized she was pregnant until last month and now, this Tuesday, a newborn slept in a sling across her breast. A secondhand Winnie-the-Pooh diaper bag was looped over her robed shoulder.

"Congratulations," Gil stated with perfectly-pitched warmth. His voice had a graveled charm he knew how to use to his advantage.

LaSalle kept her lashed gaze lowered. In all this time she had never spoken a word to him. She was modest, as befit her clothing. The cloying perfume seemed a bit over the top – but who was Gil to complain?

New Paltz was the second stop on his northbound New York City-to-Montreal shuttle. The bus was running ten minutes late. Gil paged quickly through LaSalle's ticket. It was always the same: a return schedule to Binghamton, the sizeable crossroads a hundred miles northwest of here. From New Paltz, Gil would take LaSalle twenty miles north to Kingston, where she would transfer to the westbound bus for Binghamton. He was anxious to get her on board so she could make her connection without any trouble. Eyes averted, he tore off the top sheet of her ticket and handed her the remainder.

A long slender hand darted out from the loose sleeve, like a fish from cover. Her ring finger was encircled with a thin blue wedding-band tattooed into the skin. A black inky splat interrupted the smooth back of her hand, a dark blossom on beige velvet. Gil recognized the mark. It was the smeared remnants of a visitor-stamp from the Shawangunk Correctional Facility, the only evidence of LaSalle's morning visit to the maximum-security prison just a ten-dollar cab ride from the bus station.

LaSalle was what Gill called one of his *prison widows* – a single wave in the invisible tide of wives, mothers, girlfriends, sisters making these clockwork migrations up and down the eastern rim of New York State. Some of them would be riding this bus long after Gil retired.

LaSalle's ticket swam with her hand and disappeared up her sleeve. As she swung past him, Gil inhaled. "Change in Kingston," he reminded her, as always. He never expected a reply.

This afternoon LaSalle faltered, startled. She glanced back at him, offering up a rare gaze into the agate eyes. Her cheeks were streaked with mascara, her mouth quivered. Then, just as quickly, her face spun away in a pale swirl of fabric and grasping the inside rail of the bus, she pulled herself and her baby on board.

Gil followed the trail of orchids onto the bus. His mind was wholly alert. She had made eye contact; that had never happened before. In her eyes he had read grief and a disquieting resolve.

He locked the bus door and secured the new protective shield that separated him from his passengers. The bus was not usually crowded this time of the week. His was a relatively new vehicle, the unsoiled gray upholstery not yet rubbed away. There were outlets for radio headsets on every seatback, rarely used except in bad weather or national emergencies.

Gil scanned the bus for his newest rider. Predictably, LaSalle had chosen a window seat four rows back, directly behind his cab. She was gazing out, her fine profile curtained by the hood, her lips moving. Gil's description was apt today: she was like a woman in mourning, shorn of her usual reserve. Of course she was a mother now; that alone could explain it.

Gil checked the aisle. The space between the two long rows of double seats was broken by a dangling hand here, a resting knee there. In the back, beside the bathroom, a pair of worn sneakers stuck up, tall as a pylon. Gil frowned; that was a safety violation. He glanced at his watch. If he took the time to clear the walkway, LaSalle might miss her connection.

He lowered himself behind the wheel, angling the rearview mirror that reflected his riders to get a better view of LaSalle. Then, honking twice, he trundled the bus out into the quaint college town.

The village sloped down to the river. The terraced main street teemed with students in shorts and tank tops. They overflowed the coffee shops and bookstores, tie-dye and tattoo parlors, spilling out into the street to celebrate the fine weather and the end of the school year. Gil navigated the close single-lane traffic, the brazen jay-walkers. In the passing storefront windows he caught the reflection of the bus. The long, blue rectangle skated across the glass in broken motion, the flying silver dog on its side in perpetual pursuit of its prey. Gil's gaze shifted forward. He never tired of this view. Beyond the town, on the other side of the river's broad floodplain, a long low ridge of cliffs gleamed in the sun, white and ribbed like the bleached fossils of whales. Bright clouds foamed above them. From the highest point of the mountain, a lone stone tower jutted up like the fixed needle of a compass.

At the first stoplight Gil picked up the microphone and blew into it. "This is the northbound bus to Montreal." His rap had the *basso* cadence of a late night DJ. "Making stops in Kingston. Albany. Plattsburgh. Canada. No smoking. No drinking. No cursing. No weapons. And please keep your body parts out of the aisle."

He glanced up into the mirror. The hand and knee had been withdrawn but the sneakers had not taken the hint. Gil sighed. He was not going to add to LaSalle's worries by making her late.

"Next stop Kingston," he concluded. "Change for Binghamton and all points west. Kingston in fifteen."

He hung up the mike. His practiced eye swept the seats in the mirror. Some heads were bent, reading or knitting, others thrown back dozing under headsets or ear buds. Gil watched LaSalle arch her neck.

She closed her eyes. Her arms were clasped around the ball of infant against her, as if its small weight was the only thing holding her in her seat.

Every two weeks she traveled these two hundred miles. To see a man Gil assumed was her husband, through a glass window for less than an hour. A man she might never touch again. What a waste of youth and beauty. She ought to be out enjoying herself, like these kids in the streets, Gil thought, a spike of outrage masking his jealousy. The intensity of her devotion was an enigma to him. He had just left a lover in New York City, another waited for him in Montreal. This back-and-forth working arrangement suited Gil's mercurial nature well. In his mind he had been unfaithful to both women with LaSalle.

The light turned green. Gil turned the bus north, out of town. Here, there was less traffic and fewer pedestrians along the rural road. To his left, the bony cliffs ran parallel to the two-lane highway, towering over stone-bordered pastures and orchards in bloom. After five miles or so, the cliffs broke into boulders big as houses. The rocks grew smaller and smaller, finally flattening into woods thick with white pine, oak, and at this time of year, flowering mountain laurel.

A blue-girded bridge spanned the north-flowing Walkill River. They were coming up on Rosendale. Kingston was ten more miles up the road. Gil would have to wait another two weeks to see LaSalle again. He spent so little time in her presence, yet she'd overtaken more and more of his thoughts. He felt a connection between them – a bond that, to his mind, had been confirmed by her brief, searing glance.

An upward motion in the mirror caught Gil's eye. LaSalle had stood unexpectedly. He watched her glide into the aisle, angling toward the back, toward the restroom he presumed. He released the accelerator. The bus slowed. She was using the seatbacks to brace each step, reaching hand over hand over hand. From the back she looked like a runner in slow motion undeterred by the weight of the child or the bold cocoon of cloth. As she passed the seats filled by women, Gil saw their heads bob up, one by one, to smile at her. *They don't see Muslim, they see mother,* he thought.

That thought was quickly followed by another, this one uninvited. He had not actually seen LaSalle's baby, had he? Only its round shape against her breast. She could be hiding anything in that sling, or under her robe. What did he know about her, except that she was capable of misguided loyalty? His eyes ricocheted from the mirror to the road to the mirror.

At that moment LaSalle pitched forward. One hand went around the sling; the other stopped her fall just inches from the floor. From inside the cloth her baby began to shriek. Gil's eyes returned to the road in time to brake against a curve. The bus swerved. Passengers cried out. Gil brought the bus back to the lane. He debated whether or not to pull over. LaSalle would surely miss her connection then. He blinked the overhead lights; that sometimes had a calming effect.

By now LaSalle had found her footing and scrambled up. The bathroom door closed behind her and her screaming infant. The restroom light on Gil's dashboard came on. Gil checked his mirror. The aisle was empty. He flashed with regret on the sneakers; no doubt they had caused her to stumble. He had failed her twice in one moment.

In the bathroom the baby went silent mid-cry. Gil reached again for the mike. "All right," he crooned. "Everybody just breathe."

Passengers jostled back in their seats. They whispered and grew still. No one stirred again for miles.

Gil's hands gripped the steering wheel. Sweat slid down his forehead. He raised an arm to swipe his head before the saltwater ran into his eyes. He was flooded with shame. He had made false and hurtful assumptions about LaSalle. He, a black man, who knew all too well about stereotypes. He had violated their bond – and himself in the process. It did not matter that LaSalle would never know; he had betrayed her with his thoughts.

The bus was already inside the Kingston city limits. Rows of peeling frame houses lined the streets of the shabby river town. In the distance a siren mourned.

Gil took up the mike once more. "King-ston." He pronounced it singsong. "This is Kingston."

The dingy bus station squatted in the northeast corner of a noisy intersection. Across the street was a boarded-up bank; on the other corner sat a small brick radiologist's office. Behind the station, a diner advertised Free Coffee with Doughnuts.

LaSalle's bus was parked in the loading zone along the curb. "Okay," Gil stated into the mike. "That's the Binghamton bus in Lane 2. I won't let it leave without you. The rest of you going on with me, we are here five minutes. Feel free to get out, have a smoke, stretch your legs. Do not wander from the station. Because like my ex-wife said, 'I love you but I'll leave you.' And she did."

It was a line he relied on whenever he needed to ease tension, his passengers or his own. His riders rose, chuckling, the panic of miles ago already forgotten. The bus emptied in no time.

Gil signaled the driver in Lane 2. LaSalle had not yet come out of the bathroom. After a moment, he went up the aisle, hands on his hips. He halted at LaSalle's seat. The floor was littered with white scraps scattered like colorless confetti. Gil bent to retrieve a few. His brow furrowed as he puzzled them together. They were the torn pieces of LaSalle's return ticket to Binghamton. When had she decided not to go home?

The shreds fell from his hand. Briefly Gil entertained the possibility that she was staying on the bus with him. He could make amends for his failings; he would find a place for her in Canada, he would take care of her and the child. Their life together would anchor him and from her he would learn the meaning of devotion.

Gil rapped on the bathroom door. His heart was pounding. "Mam?" He dared not call her by name, not yet. That would be a serious breach of his code.

"Are you all right?" he asked, through the door.

She did not answer. Gil looked at his watch. "This bus has to leave in four minutes," he stated, feeling foolish. He was in unmapped terrain here, where there were no traffic signs or rules to guide him.

There was no reply. "Four minutes," he repeated helplessly.

"Go away," she commanded from behind the door.

Gil held his breath. He had heard LaSalle's voice. He pivoted obediently and went back to his cab, lifting his attaché case onto the seat and shuffling tickets mindlessly. He would not take her dismissal as an insult. No, on the contrary, it felt intimate, as if she trusted him to understand her motives. Her accent was not Middle Eastern, more likely Hispanic, he noted. Another wrong assumption he had made about her.

Three minutes ticked by. His passengers re-boarded, clutching bags of chips, candy bars, and sodas. Still LaSalle did not appear. Gil went up the aisle again, pretending to count the unfilled seats. His hand was raised to knock on the restroom door when his arm halted in mid-air.

On the other side of the door LaSalle was hissing, a sound like air escaping a punctured tire. "I will not tell you this again, *cariña*." Her whisper was fierce. Who was she talking to?

"How your father wooed me and won me. How he stole me from Jesus and brought me to Allah." She could have been speaking into Gil's ear. "Well." She hissed again. "They have both abandoned us."

There was a rustle and flap of fabric. Gil put his hands on the door. He swayed on his feet. He heard LaSalle murmur, "He said he was going to die in there. He said God told him to surrender and that I must let go, or I will die also."

Gil leaned against the door. He feared for LaSalle's sanity. He prayed no one was watching. He was eavesdropping on a passenger and he could not move away. Their connection, he realized now, was as weightless as his shadow. He felt strangely bereft, as if that same shadow had suddenly deserted him. He did not know her at all. His mind jumped to the woman waiting for him in Montreal; she, at least, was real. Gil saw himself with unusual clarity: he would always be this back-and-forth man shuttling between destinations and love.

"Forget this day, *cariña*," LaSalle was whispering. "Forget everything I have told you."

The inside latch clicked. The bathroom door opened and LaSalle stepped forward. For a second she and Gil stood face-to-face, hands in the air inches apart, like dancers in a reel. Gil noted only the startled expression in her eyes before he bounded down the aisle.

At his cab he bent over the attaché case, closing it with a snap. He could feel his heart ticking against his ribs. As always LaSalle's perfume preceded her. Gil straightened. He had to say something.

"See you in two weeks –" he began. His greeting went unfinished.

LaSalle's cowl and robes were gone. She wore jeans ripped at the knee and a white off-the-shoulder lace blouse. Her arms were long and gleaming, her waist slim. The weighted sling crossed one naked shoulder, the diaper bag hung from the other. The prison stamp had been scrubbed from her hand, though the tattooed wedding ring remained.

LaSalle turned her face from Gil's confusion. A rope of ebony hair swung like a pendulum against her back as she hurried past him down the bus steps. Gil followed, his large frame filling the doorway of the bus.

"LaSalle!" he called after her. "I'm sorry."

She was already gone. All that remained was a flash of Winnie-the-Pooh bouncing around the corner of the station, and the faint sweet smell of dying orchids consumed by the fumes of the bus. Gil never saw her again.

# Lizzie Takes Roanoke

L izzie never intended to go by bus to her 40th high school reunion. She never intended to go, period. As she boarded the careworn coach panting in the gas station parking lot, Lizzie's hazel eyes glistened with mossy self-pity. She tried to re-trace the steps that had brought her to this calamity. She should never have mentioned the reunion to Ros in the first place, or the fact that the five-day nostalgic binge was being held in November this year.

Ros had not hesitated. She had a sudden strong hunch this reunion could be a game-changer for Lizzie. "Just think." Ros' voice was dry as sandpaper. "Seeing how fat, bald, and miserable the popular kids have got might be a positive thing.

Lizzie had shot Ros the Look, the squint-eyed glare that asked, *Is that supposed to be funny?* Ros had been Lizzie's kid sister for fifty-odd years and Lizzie still didn't know when she was kidding.

This time Ros was not. Lizzie had been down in the doldrums ever since her husband Morty passed suddenly, three years ago, at the age of fifty-five. Their kids were grown and elsewhere, her grandbabies were school photos on the fridge. She had stopped going to church, or bowling. When her car died last summer, she hadn't even bothered to replace it, as if making the point that there was none.

Besides, reunions terrified Lizzie. Announcements came every ten years like booster shots for diphtheria. In high school she'd been shy, invisible and – let's face it – flat-chested. Short of a boob job, she would have to make some sort of spectacular entrance, one guaranteed to make her classmates stand up and cheer. Lizzie had thrown the announcement in the trash.

But Ros kept insisting that she go. And pretty soon the idea of renting a fancy new car to drive to Roanoke rolled to the front of Lizzie's mind and parked itself there. It was no stretch to picture herself squealing up to the Patrick Henry High School gymnasium in a gleaming black Lincoln town-car convertible, curling orange and red flames painted on the side. The image brought on a hot flash, which she took for a sign.

In the end Lizzie settled for the priciest car Rent-A-Dream had to offer: a mother-of-pearl-gray Cadillac convertible with a satin maroon top and four hundred miles on the dash. Ros hadn't made a peep about the extravagance, or the five-hundred bucks Lizzie had to borrow four days before her trip. The loan would pay off part of the balance on her credit card so she'd have enough room on it for the Caddy. Ros had handed over the check without comment. Her round flat face conveyed the emotion of a frying pan. She even agreed to take Lizzie to get the car early Monday morning. Lizzie secretly suspected her little sister was curious to see the Caddy for herself.

The day had been a disaster from beginning to end but at least Lizzie looked nice. She had on make-up for once, and the slimming dove-gray suit Ros had picked out for her at Dillard's. It went well with her thick salt-and-pepper hair and the liquid green eyes, her best features by far. The matching hat had a cranberry-colored silk rose the size of a small cabbage that bobbed every time Lizzie so much as blinked. It badly needed a safety pin.

"Did you get the check in the bank?" was the first thing out of Ros' mouth that morning. Lizzie's slippery grasp of money was a constant thorn in Ros' considerable side. Lizzie nodded and bit her lip. She'd deposited the check late Friday afternoon, close to closing. That same day some nonsense from the Department of Motor Vehicles had come in the mail, some rigmarole about discontinued insurance and the license plates on her late car. She had thrown that in the trash, too, along with the reunion announcement.

The sisters dropped like twin white sandbags into the front seat of Ros' SUV and closed the doors. Lizzie flipped the visor down to check herself out in the mirror.

"I don't look ridiculous, do I?"

"Not especially." Ros felt Lizzie's laser-Look without turning her head. "What? You look fine."

Lizzie leaned back, one hand holding her hat as if she could already feel the wind on her face. "I'm going to put down the top and sail in there like a movie star."

"La de da." Ros backed the SUV out of Lizzie's driveway. "And if nobody sees you in the parking lot, you can always drive the car into the gym."

The Rent-A-Dream office was sandwiched between a Waffle House and a Red Lobster on a worn stretch of Maryland state highway. The SUV swung into the parking lot. Lizzie scanned for the Caddy. There were popsicle-colored limos, a few glammed-up Chevy Malibus, and one very impressive hot-pink Mustang convertible.

Lizzie gasped: there was the Cadillac, without a doubt the classiest car on the lot. The dark-red top was a silk umbrella over a chassis that curved like Lennox china. And the hubcaps – Lizzie had forgotten about hubcaps. These sparkled like a pimp-mobile's.

Ros shifted into park and shined her eyes at her sister. "You are going to have a fabulous time and I get to say 'I told you so.'"

The small steel-barn building that housed the Rent-A-Dream office looked misplaced beside the chichi merchandise, as if a tornado had dropped it there by accident, like Dorothy's house in Oz. It was as charmless inside as it was out. Behind a metal desk sat a red-faced sales-man, his features dominated by a thick, rusty mustache and the fat cigar protruding out from under it.

"Yeah?" he barked, without looking up from his computer. He had Spiderman Band-Aids on both his elbows.

Lizzie pointed out the window at the Cadillac. "I ordered that."

The salesman's smile reduced his eyes to slits. "Of course you did." He uncorked the cigar from his lips and placed the soggy end on the desk. "Credit card, driver's license, pu-lease."

"No prob," Lizzie boomed. She hardly knew what she was saying.

The salesman took her credit card, swiping it with professional flourish. The greased ends of his mustache sagged. "It's not going through."

Lizzie gripped the edge of the desk. The salesman ran the card again. He narrowed his eyes at the screen. "What's today? November 11th. It's Veterans' Day."

"The banks are closed." Ros' pronouncement fell on Lizzie's neck like a guillotine blade.

Lizzie swallowed. "I deposited the check on Friday." Her voice had suddenly gotten very small.

The salesman didn't miss a beat. "Then let's just call the credit card folks, why don't we, and get them to clear your account since I mean, the money – it *is* in the bank, right, lady?"

The rose on Lizzie's hat shook violently. She no longer trusted her voice. Ros plopped down on the bench, clutching her purse. The tips of her ears had turned bright red.

The man dialed a number and handed Lizzie the phone. A very agreeable woman on the other end seemed to grasp her dilemma right away. Even better, there was something she could do about it, something called a manual authorization. Lizzie thought that sounded vaguely erotic but she didn't care so long as the Caddy was still hers.

"They'll do it manually," she informed the salesman, blushing.

He smacked his chubby hands together. "I love it."

Snatching up her driver's license, he tapped the number into the computer. "Your license has been suspended."

Lizzie's thoughts went immediately to the letter from the DMV lying in her trash basket. Her heart sank. "What?" She managed to sound incredulous. "No."

The salesman's crusty eyelids drooped with doubt. Lizzie swung around to face Ros, palms in the air like someone being robbed at gunpoint.

"Don't say anything," she insisted, between clenched teeth. Grabbing her cards, she trudged out the door, the rose dangling precariously over the brim of her hat. Ros trailed behind her in disgrace.

In the parking lot Lizzie burst into tears. "Get in the car," Ros ordered. Lizzie did as she was told. They drove past the Caddy without a second glance.

Ros maneuvered into traffic. Lizzie wiped her eyes on the sleeve of her jacket. It left a clayey smudge. She rolled down the window and with one motion swept off her hat and tossed it like a Frisbee into the Waffle House parking lot.

"Well," Lizzie breathed. "That kept me from making a *complete* fool of myself."

"Bullshit," Ros replied. They rarely raised their voices anymore. "You're going."

"No, Ros," Lizzie pouted. "Not without the Caddy."

"Would you stop calling it that? You can always fly to Virginia."

"I hate flying, you know that."

"So take the train."

"Too expensive."

"Excuse me, Mrs. Caddy. Then ride the bus."

Lizzie folded her arms. "Over my dead body."

"Fine," Ros returned. "I'll ship it to the reunion. That'll make an impression."

To both their surprise, Lizzie laughed.

Back at Lizzie's, Ros made a few phone calls. Lizzie changed her clothes and took a Xanax. There was a bus to Virginia leaving late Tuesday morning but before she left Harford County, Lizzie had one more stop to make. State law required her to hand in her license *in person* at the DMV, as if the morning's Rent-A-Nightmare humiliation had not been punishment enough for whatever she had done to them.

The next day Ros drove Lizzie to the bus station. Lizzie wore a zebra-striped scarf tied under her chin. Pink rhinestone-tipped sunglasses hid the fact that she'd been crying. She had stopped resisting, as if her privileges as older sister had been turned in with her driver's license.

When they got to the bus station, it was locked and empty. No counters, no passengers, no addicts at the curb. Tattered 'For Lease' signs were taped to the doors and windows. The station had been closed for so long, there were no directions to a new station, if indeed there even was one.

"Now do you get it, Ros?" Lizzie cried. "Please, can we just go home?"

Ros would not be detoured. She went across the street to the Sonic and demanded to know where the hell the bus station had gone to. A waitress on roller blades thought she'd heard something about a gas station at the I-95 exit near Aberdeen maybe? Ros hot-rodded back into traffic.

The bus to Baltimore was idling in the BP parking lot. Ros bought Lizzie a round-trip ticket to Roanoke, checked her bags, and herded her, grumbling, onto the bus. Lizzie found a seat by a window. Moisture clouded the pane but she could still make out Ros waving to her from the parking lot. Lizzie didn't return her waves, nor did she follow the SUV with her eyes when it drove out of sight.

Under Lizzie's knees the engine was rumbling so hard she could feel it vibrating in her stomach. The seats were small and too close together, the upholstery grimy and rough. Above her head, the underside of a baggage rack had buttons for a reading light and a little round vent for air. She would definitely need more air. The smell was nauseating – a sour mix of unwashed bodies, fried food, sweat, grease, urine, and a useless swipe of ammonia. Half-eaten chicken bones wrapped in a napkin were crammed into the mesh sack on the back of the seat in front of her. Her shoes stuck to the floor, as if to prevent her escape. An open can of soda sloshed against her left foot.

Lizzie's hand found a lever between her seat and the wall. She prayed it was an ejection button. As she pulled it, the seat slammed backwards, leaving her staring up at the air vent, gawking back at her like a loose eyeball. She pushed the lever down and the seat flew upright, bringing her face-to-face with an embroidered pack of red, blue and yellow greyhounds racing across the seatback. Over the dogs Lizzie could see the double rows of seats, each rounded with the crown of a head like candies in a box of assorted nuts. Lizzie felt more like an anchovy, crammed in with strangers in a small metal can. She thought hell would be preferable to this. Or maybe this *was* hell. Her former pastor had described the lower regions as hot and crowded; that pretty much summed up her current situation. Thank God the seat beside her was still empty.

The bus began backing out of its parking bay. Lizzie gripped the arm rest. A stick-thin, older fellow came scurrying down the aisle and dropped into the unfilled space beside her. His limbs jerked up and down like a Pinocchio on strings. His legs flopped into the aisle.

"I crazy," he announced.

Lizzie wasn't sure: was this a warning, or just an observation? She thought she detected an Oriental accent and alcohol on his breath. She waited for the man to say more. When he didn't, the silence began to harden. Lizzie felt it was her job to shatter it.

"It's all my fault," she began. "I could have avoided all this." Her gesture took in the bus, the old man, and her uncertain future.

"I shouldn't of hit up Ros for that extra five hundred," she admitted. "That was my mistake. Then? I waited too long. Didn't get it in till late Friday and who remembers Veterans' Day? Morty, that's who."

Lizzie's eyes threatened rain again. Three years later, it still hurt to think about Morty and the shocking way he had died. She missed his noisy eating habits, his quiet adoration of her. Sex had been their glue. Many nights in her empty bed she had asked God to let her join him, but it seemed that God, like so many of their married friends, was less interested in her now that she was no longer a package deal.

She glanced over at the old man. Not five minutes out of town and she was already spilling her guts to a total stranger. It was the bus, it had to be. All this togetherness was squeezing the words out of her like toothpaste from a tube. Or maybe it was the Xanax.

"And my license?" she scoffed, unable to stop. "Please. Just because I dropped the insurance when the car died and sent in the plates two months later? What, they take your license for that? Excuse me. People spend their lives thinking these things up?"

The old man's eyes were closed. He had gotten very still. Lizzie stole another sideways peek. She had a secret thing for Asian men, ever since as a teenager, she'd seen Don Ho sing on TV. This guy wasn't bad-looking; he just needed a haircut and a 12-step program.

The old man's eyes popped open. He put out a gnarled paw. "You want hold hand?"

Lizzie was shocked. "What?" She flushed. "No! Sir, have you been drinking?"

"Me-di-ca-tion!" he shouted. He puckered his lips. "How bout kiss?"

"No!"

Heads turned their way. "Stop it!" Lizzie lowered her voice. "Behave yourself or I'll – I'll – I don't know what I'll do."

The old man snickered. "You crazy!" he barked, and fell back asleep.

Lizzie exhaled the breath she was holding. She fanned herself with the ends of her scarf. She hadn't been this near a man in how many years? What if she had a hot flash? She dared not remove a stitch of clothing in front of this fellow. Reaching up to open the air vent, Lizzie found herself wishing she'd gone to an earlier reunion, one when she was younger, before her body from every angle resembled the capital letter B. And she thought of something else, too. That years ago she used to dream of showing up at a high school reunion in a long white limo with ten gorgeous Asians in white karate robes and six elegant white wolfhounds in tow. She didn't know how the wolfhounds had wormed their way into her fantasy; she and Morty had a Schnauzer. But here she was, going to Roanoke on a Greyhound bus in the company of one horny Chinaman.

The bus had a layover at the Baltimore Travel Plaza. The signs to the Women's Room guided Lizzie past the arcade games and the vending machines. They led her around one corner after another until she came to the wide arched doorway of the large black-and-white tiled ladies' bathroom. Directly in her path was a young black woman talking excitedly on her cell phone. The woman's bosom and buttocks were balanced on her small frame with breathtaking symmetry. Lizzie swerved in time to avoid collision. The young woman was intent on her phone conversation. Lizzie could have sworn she heard her say something like *byhfuckyoubyh* before she snapped the phone shut.

Lizzie hurried into a stall. When she peered back, the young woman had vanished. Lizzie locked the door and brought out some handy-wipes she'd thought to bring along. She scrubbed the toilet seat and then squatted over it like a hovercraft anyway, just in case. The toilet had a sensor on it that flushed before she was finished, as if it knew something she didn't.

At midnight Lizzie re-boarded the bus. Don Ho was not in his seat. In his place slept a handsome black lady in a gray sweat suit and jingly earrings. Lizzie panicked: was she on the wrong bus? No, there was her leopard-print carry-on in the window seat where she'd left it. She stepped carefully past the lady's knees. Her new seatmate was very pretty and very pregnant.

Fortunately the lady slept. Lizzie didn't know how a person could sit so comfortably for so long with essentially a bowling ball on her lap. She herself found it impossible to sleep. Where was she supposed to put her hands? Or her feet? She flipped from side to side and tried not to feel too sorry for herself. It was like trying to sleep on a Magic-Motion-Bed with no off-button. She dozed once or twice.

Around two Lizzie woke to the unmistakable voice of the young woman from the Baltimore bathroom shouting, "Who you calling a ho? Who you calling a ho?" At first Lizzie thought she was dreaming about Don. She heard cries of "Hush!" Shouts of "You tell it, sister!" She was amazed her seatmate could sleep through all this mayhem. She had to be dreaming after all.

The agitated voice was directly behind her. It sounded like the young woman was on her cell phone again. "You ask Diddy," she demanded. "*I'm* the one with the condo. *You* the one with the baby." A moment of silence, and the young woman replied, "My skin is lovely. Your skin is garbage."

"I don't need to know your business, girl." The lady beside Lizzie had spoken up without moving a muscle. Her tone was that of someone used to being obeyed.

"I got to go," the young woman whispered. "Bye. Fuck you. Bye." The cell phone clapped close. "You people need to refresh," she announced as if speaking to children, and the bus grew still again.

For a minute Lizzie almost missed Ros; at the least she would have stories to tell her. She tried once more to get comfortable. The next hour passed slowly. At 3 am her seatmate woke with a start, patting her mound of belly.

"I already got two of these," the lady whispered, by way of introduction. "A boy and a girl. They handful enough."

Lizzie rolled her eyes. "Been there. Done that."

"Right? I thought I was done with babies." In confidential tones the lady recounted to Lizzie how she'd gone to her doctor to get her tubes tied. "There I was, up on the table, legs flapping in the breeze, when she told me I was pregnant and sent me on home!"

A shake of the lady's head sent her earrings jigging. She dropped her voice. "You never know. And me being a nurse and all, you think I would. Now look at me, big as my aunt's booty and due next week. My daughter? Serena? She's ten. She excited. She wants a little sister."

"I got one of those," Lizzie answered. "She's the reason I'm sitting here."

The lady smiled and patted Lizzie's knee. "No, baby. Jesus is the reason you're sitting here."

Jesus apparently was also to blame for sending the lady back to her doctor for a sonogram. "And I'm telling you, this baby ain't no sister. Uh-uh." She poked a finger in the air. "Its manly thing was just wa-aving."

She leaned into Lizzie. "So then I got this idea to play a trick on my daughter." The lady brought the sonogram home for Serena to see. Told her she had gotten her wish: the baby was going to be a girl. Serena had peered at the image for a long, long time.

"Finally she looks up at me," the lady recalled. "And she goes, 'Mami? This baby going to be gay.'"

Lizzie laughed out loud. The lady chuckled. "Uh-huh. That's what my husband did too. Sputted out his coffee all over the kitchen table – "

She stopped in mid-sentence. Her gaze emptied out as if her eyes had backed up and dropped down inside her. Lizzie heard a champagne bottle cork pop. A warm liquid gushed to the floor, splattering her pants legs.

The lady grabbed Lizzie's hand. "My water broke." Her face twisted with the first contraction. "Sweet Jesus, I'm going to have this baby on the bus!"

Lizzie looked around. "Shouldn't we tell someone?"

From behind her came the young woman's voice. "We know."

"Tell anybody you want to!" the lady cried. "It's coming now!" She squeezed down on Lizzie's fingers. "Ever deliver a baby before?"

"I've never been on a bus before!" Lizzie's squeal hit high notes of terror.

"Nothing to it!" the lady squeaked back. She was already turning her body and pushing Lizzie out of the seat with her feet.

The bus driver came on the loudspeaker, his voice big as God's. "Any doctors on board?" His question produced swells of laughter, one shout of "I'm a Doctor of Funk!" but alas, no medical doctors.

The lady clung to Lizzie's fingers. "I love you!" she cried. Her hand shot into the air. "I love everybody!"

The rest of that ride would always remain slightly fuzzy to Lizzie. The bus driver *did* manage to get the lady to the nearest hospital – but not before her impatient baby boy had slished into Lizzie's hands.

She pulled off her scarf and bundled it around the bus' newest passenger. She was trembling with awe and estrogen. The last time she'd felt this alive was the last time she and Morty made love. They had just finished and were drifting into sleep when Morty gave out a broken howl and died in her arms. She had never told anyone, not even Ros; it was too private, too horrible, too sad. He went in his sleep, was the story she told, which was true more or less. For three years she had wondered if she killed him. Now, cradling the squalling baby in her arms, Lizzie felt an unexplicable lightness, as though she'd dropped twenty pounds of guilt at the cleaners. Birth and death were alike; they could both surprise you. It was good that Morty went that way, even if it was much too soon. His death was their last, best secret.

She handed the baby to his sobbing mother. The lady squashed Lizzie's face with her fingers and kissed her on the lips. Everybody around them was laughing and crying, high-fiving and hugging all at the same time.

The bus was half-a-day behind schedule when it finally arrived in Roanoke late Wednesday afternoon. The 'Welcome Class of '72' was due to start in the high school gym in less than two hours. Lizzie stepped off the bus into the warmish autumn sun. She put on her sunglasses. She was messy and smelly and basically done. She was seriously thinking about taking the next bus back to Maryland.

Roanoke had been her home for three unhappy years and she'd never been in its bus station. She felt a curious stab of regret, as if that one omission might have given those years the luster they lacked. The building had been newly remodeled inside and out, nicely-tiled, freshly painted. The old payphone on one wall was all that remained of the station's former dilapidation. Absently, Lizzie bought a *Roanoke Times*, folding it under her arm to read on the way home. She had a sudden impulse to call Ros. Luckily, neither the bank nor the DMV had taken her phone card.

Ros picked up on the second ring. "This better be you." Her voice sounded shivery.

"Ros, you're not going to believe this."

"I believe it!" Ros' excitement jumped through the phone. "Lizzie, you're famous!"

Lizzie shot Ros the Look through the phone. "I'm not kidding!" Ros exclaimed. "You're on the front page of every national newspaper!"

"What?" Lizzie grabbed the newspaper under her arm. Oh my God, there she was, on the bus, she and the radiant new mother lip-to-lip with the zebra-swathed infant between them. The picture had been taken on the cell phone of the young woman with the real estate and the good skin.

"It went viral on the Internet." Ros was practically bubbling.

A large chattering group came into the station. Annoyed, Lizzie put a finger to one ear. A middle-aged blonde at the front of the crowd waved in her direction, the limp white skin of her underarm flapping like a truce flag. Lizzie waved back with her fingers, certain the woman had made a mistake.

"Lizzie!" the blonde woman shrieked and bounded over, tanned cleavage heaving. Lizzie stared. In her wake were forty or so of her former classmates, still recognizable even if they were all fat, bald and miserable. At the moment they were smiling at Lizzie and clapping. A few of them held up her front-page photo. Others carried signs that read "Welcome home, Lizzie" and "Lizzie Delivers!" It was better than she'd pictured it.

Royalty could not have waved more grandly than Lizzie at that moment. "I got to go," she whispered to Ros, lowering the phone.

"Lizzie!" Ros shouted.

Lizzie brought the receiver to her ear. "What?"

"I just wanted to say, 'I told you so.'"

Lizzie laughed. "Bye. Fuck you. Bye," she said, and hung up.

# Graceland

It happened every time she waited for the bus to Memphis to depart. As the bus sat idling in its lane, a peddler would come up the aisle, silently dropping small articles into each passenger's lap. Last trip she'd gotten a key chain with a blue plastic dolphin attached. The two-dollar price tag read: *I am deaf. Please buy this item so I can eat. Thank you. God bless you.*

She had only ten dollars to feed herself until she got home. And she couldn't help wonder if the deaf-mute thing wasn't really a scam; the peddler's unresponsive demeanor was almost *too* convincing. But that didn't keep her from purchasing whatever was put in her hand.

Last year she'd given the blue-dolphin chain to a dark-eyed little boy sitting across the aisle from her. He kept peeking out from behind an old man whose face resembled a withered brown leaf. The woman couldn't tell if the child was just curious, or wanting to play. She hoped, by giving him the dolphin, he would forget she was there. By this time – the home stretch of her journey – she was all peopled out.

Today's key chain had a crucifix dangling from its ring. The silver-plated cross was about three inches long and two inches wide with Jesus' half-clothed body hung across it. She liked its weight in her hand. Growing up *Hebrew* – as the Carolina Mountain folk called their smattering of local Jews – Jesus had been a confusing presence in her life, a sort of esteemed distant cousin whose birthday you had to ignore.

But the music He inspired – gospel, shape note, and blue grass – was all around and felt like hers. Song itself was the Divine, transcending ancestry and allegiances, even to God.

She counted out two dollars. Instantly, the peddler appeared above her, his spotted almond cheeks topped by shoe-polish black hair. He took her money, nodding without smiling, and hurried down the aisle, plucking unsold chains from the passengers' outstretched hands.

The crucifix went in her purse. She considered taking out her anti-quated CD player, though she preferred the dark for that. She didn't like calling attention to herself on the bus. Which was absurd really. A gray-haired white woman could not have been more unremarkable among the well-dressed, elderly blacks and Latinos, the gorgeous young people with their tattooed muscles and pierced midriffs, the still-younger soldiers, boys and girls, confident in their cool desert camouflage.

The bus grumbled to a start and lumbered into downtown Dallas. The streets were narrow as river canyons between sheer walls of concrete and glass. The mirrored buildings reflected a dozen red-ball sunrises simmering on the horizon. In time, the city gave way to the eastbound highway bordered in swaths of bluebonnet, bull thistle, Indian paint-brush. The sky was an empty, over-turned bowl, its white ceramic glaze baked on by the urgent heat of late May.

Every spring she made this same circular route. From her home in Birmingham she went north and east to her parents' grave in the Smokey Mountains, then up to the Great Lakes to see her sister, fol-lowed by a visit with her kid brother's family in Denver, and ending in east Texas with a sister-in-law leftover from a brief early marriage. They all had children now – grandchildren some of them – steady jobs and social lives so they counted on her to come see them. That was fine; her life was so interior it was easy for others to miss.

Each time she swore she'd never do it again. Fifty-six was getting a little old for the long nights of broken sleep, the endless string of smoke breaks at McDonalds. What would happen if she stopped visiting her family every year? She would become that distant relative whose birthday you forgot.

It had not escaped her notice that for fifteen years the bus had provided her only possibilities of romance. She'd been proposed to four times, once by a blue-black West African who vowed to wait for her; she couldn't remember his name. The other names were interchangeable, Carlos or Juan, belonging to slim-hipped young men who gravitated to her like tiny tan hawks with a predator's eye for middle-aged women traveling alone.

She parked her backpack in the empty seat beside her. Then leaning her head against the dusty windowpane, she let the countryside roll out like frames of grainy film – pasture by pasture, trailer by trailer, billboard by billboard.

* * *

The old man was perched on a wooden bench under a tattered poster for Lucky Strikes. He'd been sitting outside the store for quite a while, waiting for the eastbound bus. His legs were hurting him again and he needed to take a leak.

His daughter-in-law had dropped him off here three hours ago. First, they had grabbed a bite at the local barbecue. The sun was low in the west when she let him out at the dilapidated general store and hurried back up the mountain. The store had locked its door shortly thereafter and he'd been alone here ever since.

The bus from Dallas was late, as usual. A warm breeze swayed the tall catalpas that shaded the weathered shack by day. A single streetlight shone by the dirt pull-off to the store. The overcast night sky gave off an eerie, orange glow. He could see across the road into a furrowed field, shiny with new crop. A ways back, a house lamp, faint as foxfire, shone through the trees. Behind them, the sleeping hills rose up black and still. It was so quiet he could have been the only one around for miles.

The old man burped. The barbecue was still working him; *that* had been a mistake. He pulled a pouch of chewing tobacco from his pants pocket, a guilty pleasure he wouldn't have dared had his wife been with him. Stuffing a pinch in the hinge of his jaw, he closed the pouch and returned it to his pocket. He'd have to remember to toss it out in the station in Memphis.

After a moment he pushed against the bench and stood, twisting his torso to steady himself against the wall. Wincing with pain, he began to limp to and fro across the gravel, stopping only to catch his breath. In the circle of light, he was ghostly white and almost as wide as he was tall. His arms were bulky, the muscle gone to fat.

His legs were a constant struggle: sit a little, walk a little. He was more than ready for the bus. The wait here had been the hardest stretch so far. He turned west to listen for traffic, and then unzipped his trousers and relieved himself by the road. If the bus came now, he would be caught with his pants down, so to speak. He had to flag the bus anyway. Surely *that* would get the driver's attention.

He zipped up, chuckling. It was a good story, even if it never happened. He needed something cheerful to take home to the wife, something other than the report that the tulips she'd planted on their son's grave had come up again this spring. Or that the boy's widow was going to re-marry and move to California. It had been four years since their son's remains were buried here in the Ozarks as he'd requested, to be close to his young wife, the daughter-in-law they inherited when he was killed. The old man shook his head. He had a feeling they'd seen the last of *that* whacko. It was better his wife didn't come this time. Losing their only child was making them old in a hurry.

He thrust his hand into his sweater pocket, his fingers seeking the lapel pin he'd stolen from the girl. The thing had leapt into his hand when he spied it under her couch. It was a little problem he'd had as a youngster: a tie clip here, a fountain pen there. He'd even spent a few nights in jail for petty theft. Meeting his wife – *that* was what brought him around. He hadn't stolen anything but kisses for decades.

But this was different. Under the streetlamp, the gold torch and black-enamel letters of his son's ROTC button needed only rubbing on his sleeve to make it shine like new. The pin had been lost, forgotten – what was his crime? It belonged to them anyway. He pinned it to the collar of his sweater. He would tell his wife the daughter-in-law had sent it to her. She would like that.

The old man heard the bus before he saw its lights swinging around the curve. He began to pump his arms like stiff-boned wings. The headlights fell on him, and the bus to Memphis came roaring up behind them. The driver blinked the lights to let the old man know he'd been seen. The old man hobbled back to the bench to gather his shopping bag of belongings, stopping only once to spit out the clotted mat of chaw.

* * *

The woman knew immediately the old man was going to sit next to her. Her overhead light was on, her mind settled pleasantly with a crossword puzzle. The old man had boarded at some nameless wayside stop and was listing down the aisle in the dark toward her.

He didn't ask if the seat beside her was taken. He just turned and backed toward it, lowering his behind as he came. The woman yanked her backpack away in time and scrunched against the window to make room for him. He was broader than a single seat; his thigh jammed up against hers. They bent in one motion – she to slide her pack under the seat, he to stuff his shopping bag under his. He kicked it out of sight and grunted.

"I got a long way to go yet."

The woman nodded. She returned to her puzzle.

"Where you going?" His voice had an odd, croaking quality.

Her eyes did not leave the page. "Alabama."

"You got a long way too."

She nodded again and brought her pencil down on a square. He was one of those, going to talk no matter what.

"You look familiar." The old man had not expected to say that.

The woman turned away, frowning at the puzzle. The old man understood. His wife worked the crosswords, too, and he knew how *she* could get. He shifted his shoulders. After a moment, his breath slowed to faint snores, sharp as hiccups.

The woman shook her head. She'd never understand how anyone could sleep so soundly so close to a total stranger, especially when you were both dressed and sober. She squeezed her lips together to keep from laughing, then looked at the sleeping old man directly.

His face was in shadow. The faint fan of light revealed only dark trousers patched at the knee. Short thick fingers were laced over his protruding belly. A small gilded pin glittered on his collar. The navy wool sweater was too warm for the season but just right for the crisp bus air-conditioning. He had traveled this way before.

The old man jerked up, gave out a queer little shriek and fell back asleep. The woman closed the puzzle book. She reached up noiselessly and turned off the light. The waning moon was yellow, tilted like broken crockery spilling melted butter. She could see the old man's face better by the moon. He looked familiar to her, too. The flat-planed cheeks, the great wiry red-and gray eyebrows and prominent hooked nose, gave him the look of the owl that roosted on her chimney in autumn. It was a face you could miss in a crowd, but up close it was unforgettable.

The bus was utterly quiet. Reaching into her purse for the CD player, the woman's fingers found the crucifix. Lifting it up, she pulled off the price tag. In the opaque light she could just make out the silver-thorned crown, the invaded ribs, the folds of His loincloth. She put the Savior back in her purse and rummaged around for her current road CD: Emmylou Harris' gospel album. *Angel Band.*

\* \* \*

"Look at that old moon."

The old man had woken with a cry, fleeing a dream. He gazed across the woman out the window. "Makes me miss my wife."

He straightened his trousers at the knees. He always made a point of mentioning the missus to any female, young or old, he met in his travels, especially in such close quarters.

The woman's eyes were closed. She pointed to the earphones. The old man stole a glance at her. Her frizzled hair was tied back from sharp-angled cheeks and parched-looking lips. Lucky for him she was no bigger than a flea.

He gazed at his hands. "I wanted her to come with me," he rasped. "But she was too poorly.

"Her stomach," he explained, after a pause. "Had an operation two weeks ago. I hated to leave her but." He swallowed. "I had my ticket, she said go."

He peeked out from under his brows as if to make certain the woman approved his logic. She pointed patiently at the earphones.

"Been down to see my son," he stated finally. He tapped the pin on his collar. "He was in Iraq."

The woman tossed her hands in the air; she gave up. She stopped the disc and laid the earphones deliberately around her neck. "Where you headed?" she asked him.

"Illinois. Get home tomorrow afternoon."

"Change in Memphis?"

His head rocked up and down. "Home of the King."

She winced inwardly. They would be joined at the hip for several more hours.

"It ain't easy for me," the old man went on. "I had two operations myself. One for the throat. The eslophagus."

The woman squeezed her lips together. The old man stroked his neck and chest. "Oh yeah. And on my legs. Look. They're still swollen."

He lifted the cuff of his pants to show her a pillar-like leg. The skin was pushed out, taut and colorless. The woman cringed in sympathy.

"It was much worse." He dropped the cloth. "I need to go back to church is what I need to do. Let the Lord work on me a while."

He went on to tell her about his wife, about the various body parts they'd each had removed, about the tarpaper shack they shared in the flatlands with a gimpy old Chihuahua named Spike. He used to be a heating and air salesman, and a good one at that.

The woman's eyelids began to flutter. She pushed herself up in the seat. Her hands gripped the headset encircling her neck.

The old man shook himself. "I'm talking your ear off."

"No, no!" She clapped a hand over her mouth. Without another word, she sank back in the seat, lowered the earphones over her ears and rolled on her side away from him.

"All right." He wove his fingers over his belly. "I don't mind. I'll sit here and watch over you. Me and the moon. You'll be like my own little daughter to me."

The old man felt an unusual sense of peace. He couldn't wait to tell his wife about the woman he'd met on the bus. He could see how it would go: the two would become close, exchanging crosswords, writing letters, eventually a phone call every Sunday, happy reunions at Christmas. You never knew what would make his wife want to live.

*  *  *

The woman opened her eyes. The bus was crossing the Mississippi River. The bridge was strung with lights, each arch making a luminescent hoop for the bus to pass through. On the black water below, the starry reflections undulated like phosphorescent snakes.

Her mouth was wet. She wiped the corner of her lips. The old man had put his shopping bag on his lap; he looked to be asleep. She dragged her pack from under the seat and put the CD player away.

The bus was curving off the Interstate into the neon throb of downtown Memphis. *Home of the King*, the old man had said. It had been a long time since she let herself think about her first introduction to Memphis. On that short-lived, windblown honeymoon.

A hollowness opened up inside her then, hovering somewhere between longing and dread. Her new husband had been a rockabilly musician. She'd known him less than three weeks when they married and embarked on a careening tour through Elvis country. First stop: Memphis, on the King's 40th birthday.

The one thing she could recall about Graceland – Elvis' redneck palace – was his guitar-shaped swimming pool; that, and the hit of acid she and her husband had shared beside it. The rest of her memories were shattered images: she and her husband singing outside the King's castle gates; a crowd of onlookers, a kid maybe; some coins in her husband's guitar case. It all got pretty confused when the cop showed up and chased them away. Vaguely she recalled money spilling from the open case as they ran. She could hear the clink of coins on the sidewalk and their wild laughter as they scooped up what change they could.

The old man woke and stretched, distracting her from her memories. She had a dim notion she'd been rude to him. The bus was already pulling into the station, the driver exhorting his passengers to stay seated until the vehicle came to a complete stop.

The woman reached into her purse. "You know what?" she told the old man. "I think I got this for you."

She held out the crucifix. The old man tilted his head toward it, his eyes rheumy and astonished. He slipped the cross into the breast pocket of his sweater and then grabbed her hand and kissed it. The stubble of his beard grazed her skin. She pulled away as if she'd received a small electric shock.

"I'm going to tell my wife about you," he explained.

The bus braked and stopped. They swayed forward. All around them people jumped to their feet, hastily pulling belongings from the overhead racks. The old man raised himself up out of his seat and the push of passengers, eager to get off, carried him down the aisle without another word.

\* \* \*

Inside the station the old man leaned against the wall. The crucifix gleamed on his palm. He could hardly wait to phone his wife and tell her what had happened. He'd have to explain why he'd kissed another woman's hand; maybe *that* could wait till she'd seen the cross for herself. Reaching into his pocket for some telephone change, he came upon the pouch of chewing tobacco. It would feel good to throw it away: one less thing he'd have to confess.

The waiting room was spacious, open as a warehouse. Along one wall were lockers-to-rent, no longer in use. September 11th had put an end to that. Anyone could stuff a bomb in a duffel bag and leave it in a locker. There were no trash cans either, for the same reason. His son had been killed in the battle for Falujah, so the old man didn't need convincing.

The station was loud tonight. At the far end was a bank of payphones. A large pale teenage girl was yelling into a phone. A child bucked in her arms, screaming, "No, no, no!" The old man shook his head. His wife would never be able to hear over that commotion. Between him and the payphones were rows of uncomfortable metal chairs. He'd gotten too big to fit in them. His bus didn't leave for three hours, so he'd have to amuse himself in the gift shop, or the greasy spoon. At least there he could sit and rest his legs. He ducked into the men's room to relieve his bladder and his conscience of the damning pouch of chaw.

When the old man returned to the waiting room, the child was still wailing. He searched the seats for the woman from the bus. In the center of the room a drunken couple was arguing. The woman wore short-shorts, a halter top and house slippers. She had white freckled skin and bleached blonde hair. The way her arms sliced the air when she yelled reminded the old man of his daughter-in-law. He cut a wide path around her.

Beside the ticket counter a young black cop was eying the rambunctious pair. His hips were hung with a gun, manacles, radio, and nightstick. The old man's son had been a cop in Cairo, and a member of the National Guard. Suddenly he remembered the stolen ROTC pin on his collar. He hoped he didn't look guilty.

He nodded at the cop and began to whistle. He whistled as he checked the schedule board above the counter. The bus to Alabama didn't depart until 3am. Surely he'd run into the woman again before then. He didn't even know her name.

In the narrow entrance to the café, tattooed teens crowded around flashing video games. Behind them a zigzag of bleary travelers waited to order burgers and pick up fries. The woman wasn't in the line, or sitting at any of the tables. Limping over to the gift shop, he found it empty, except for the shapely black girl behind the register. She was on her cell phone. Her red apron dripped with all manner of bling: ribbons and buttons and whatnots.

The old man slowed. He would browse here a while. There might even be a trinket in it for his wife, though nothing could compare to the gift in his pocket. He pressed his fingers against the crucifix to make sure it was there, and real. He gazed around the shop. Stuffed greyhounds paraded along the upper shelves. His wife liked that kind of thing, but a fake dog would make Spike jealous. The earrings and bracelets in the display counter were nice but too costly. He spun the rack of puzzle books, cheap paperbacks, and religious self-help. A gift to make her laugh would be better: googly-eyed sunglasses, an Elvis knickknack, a silly sign with a bow-legged mule.

Overpriced picture-postcards celebrated the mighty Mississippi, Memphis' infamous Beale Street music, and the city's rock-and-roll shrine, Graceland. He picked up a card with Elvis' cockamamie pool on the front. He'd seen it for himself. On a sightseeing trip they'd taken to Memphis, when their little boy was four or five. The first morning they'd gone down to the Peabody Hotel so the kid could see the famous Marching Ducks making their daily parade through the lobby on a red carpet rolled out just for them. The child had laughed and clapped his hands as the birds sauntered like celebrities all the way to the marble fountain where they would spend their day. But you never knew what would stick with a kid. The whole way back to Illinois, the only thing the boy talked about was the cop outside Graceland. It was Elvis' 40th birthday, and the policeman was shooing away a couple of singing hippies, a man and a woman in ragtag tie-dye. The scruffy musicians had scrambled off, laughing, the few coins they earned falling from a guitar case. The officer had picked up the change and given it to the kid. The boy didn't care about the money; he only saw the cop, his gun, the radio. He talked about that radio for months. He was hooked even then. Yeah, thirty-five was too young to give up your life, but at least his son died doing what he was born to do. If that wasn't success, the old man didn't know what was. Try explaining that to the boy's mother.

He saw it all clearly now. There was a Divine hand in how things happened. You could trust it, even if you didn't like it. For years, he'd been drifting from the Lord. Now his King had called him back. He need not fear his wife's death or his own, nor mourn his son a second longer. They would all be together one day soon, of that he had just been reassured.

He had to find the woman. But what would he say to her? Thank-you was not enough. The thought of kissing her hand made his cheeks burn with amazement and dismay. He'd have to give the Lord credit for that, too.

What could he give her in exchange? That was it. He'd get something for her instead of the wife. He had fifteen bucks, enough for a phone call and three meals. For a second he considered giving the woman his son's ROTC pin, but that didn't sit so well with him. There had to be something else.

His eye fell on a rack of key chains with Elvis ornaments attached: a cardboard guitar, a plastic replica of Graceland complete with columns, a bust of the King himself. A gold-plated chain came with a portrait of Elvis in a flashing gold frame. He was dressed all in white, a single molten spotlight behind him, his knees bent, his hips thrust forward. It was perfect. He would trade her chains. Jesus for Elvis, a King for a King.

He flipped the portrait over. $14.95. He could afford it, if he didn't call his wife. Or eat. You had to buy food to sit at the café tables or otherwise the cop would move you along. Buying anything in the store would mean standing or walking for the next three hours. He had to sit at least part of the time, someplace other than the john.

Unless he stole it. The idea was out in his mind before he could stop it. He cut his eyes at the cash register. The blinged-out clerk was no longer on her cell. She was leaning on the counter, her head propped up on one hand, practically asleep. It would be so easy to slip a small item into his pocket and walk away. He pressed his hand against the crucifix. *Help me.*

\* \* \*

Memphis was the woman's least favorite stop on the whole go-around. In the middle of the night, the station was at its surliest. By the payphones a little boy howled in the clutch of an overweight teenager. Neither of them looked like they got very much sunlight. A pair of drunks in the middle of the room was a different disaster. The blonde was passed out across two chairs, revealing an ugly gash above a bruised eye. Her partner, a rail-thin guy with a gray pompadour, leaned over her, shouting into her face. They felt combustible, as if at any second they might burst into flame.

The woman skirted the smoldering couple, the flailing child. Just as she passed the on-duty cop, she glanced back. The blonde came to suddenly, spit in the pompadour's face, and raced out the station's glass doors. The woman retreated into the doorway of the gift shop as the pompadour marched past her after the blonde, his hands swinging like paddles, and the cop fell in behind them, pursuing them onto the street.

The woman turned into the gift shop. It never seemed to change from year to year. The same dingy stuffed animals still lined the shelves; the books in the racks had the same musty smell. She halted. Ten feet away, the old man was bent over a display counter. She backed out of the shop before he could spot her.

In the waiting room, the child was still shrieking, "No! No!" over the teen's desperate shouts. The woman peered past the dinging video games into the busy café. Her head ached from lack of sleep and food. She whirled around, not knowing where to go, and then pushed through the front doors of the station.

In fifteen years of Memphis layovers she'd never been outside. The drunks and the cop were nowhere to be seen. The bus depot was in the heart of the hotel section, surrounded by smoky music clubs and all-night places to eat. Down the street, in the circular driveway of a Radisson Inn, sat a huge plastic hot dog in a vinyl-shiny roll. It was as big as a cement truck. The marquee above the frank read: *Pork Products Trade Show. Come In and Pig Out.*

Laughter spiraled up the street. On the far sidewalk two young musicians were trailed by two young women in low-cut tops and jeans. The men's shoulders were bent under the weight of guitars and amplifiers. They wore their ambition like logos on T-shirts. Memphis had not changed that much, either.

All at once, a dented town car with a missing back fender screeched around the corner and pulled up to the curb. The teenage girl rushed out of the station, carrying the now-sleeping boy. The door slammed. The car squealed up the street through a red light and vanished.

The woman breathed into the quiet. Soft mist circled the streetlights with haloes. She could still feel the scrape of the old man's beard on her hand. The intrusion of his kiss – *that* wasn't what bothered her. She didn't envy him his love for his wife, or his wife his dependable loyalty. What had rattled her was the exultation she'd glimpsed on his face when she held out the crucifix to him. That transfixed joy, its transparent purity – when had she ever felt anything like that?

Across the street the musicians were cracking wiener jokes and making the girls giggle. Their voices went right into her. She'd known it once, if only for a moment, in the merger of her husband's voice with hers. Somewhere in this maze of streets was the dark corner where he had scored a bag of heroin the third day of their honeymoon. She scarcely remembered the perilous ride from Memphis to the east Texas town where he'd left her with his sister. But she never forgot his parting words. *If you can't be an artist, at least live an artist's life.*

Well, she had failed at both. From Texas she went to New York City to make it as a singer. The auditions were packed; the callbacks caused her to throw up. This wasn't how music was supposed to make her feel. She packed her bags and went home to the Smokeys. She didn't have the courage to make the necessary sacrifices. But when her parents got sick, she made sacrifices anyway, and stayed with them ten years. Somewhere along the way, she stopped singing.

The old man's rapture haunted her. She had not just abandoned the effort to make her life count; she no longer cared if it did. She'd become indifferent to the possibility that her life could matter, if not to anyone else, then to herself lying alone in the dark when the hollowness descended.

The coronas around the streetlights sharpened, refracted by her tears. A soft rain began to fall. She held her palms up to receive the drops. The asphalt was shiny as patent leather. On the sidewalk across the street, traces of warm footsteps evaporated in the cool wet air.

After a moment she realized she was hungry. She went back inside the station. The cop had returned to his post by the ticket counter. She walked into the café. The cold air was dry as paper. She bought a box of popcorn and a Dr. Pepper, and glanced around for somewhere to sit.

A raised hand got her attention. The old man sat in a booth facing the door. He waved her over. On the table before him was a feast of burgers, French fries, and oozy orange nachos.

"I got something for you," he croaked.

The woman slid into the seat across from him and dug into her popcorn. The old man held out a closed fist, like a child playing a guessing game. She offered her palm and he dropped her gift into it. Her fingers curled around metal and plastic. She opened her hand. Perched on her palm was a key chain with a miniature plastic Graceland, columns and all.

She choked and coughed, took a sip of soda. "Where did you get this?" she asked him.

"I want you to know I didn't steal it." The old man tapped the empty lapel where his son's ROTC pin had been. "I traded the girl. She likes that kind of thing."

The woman had no idea what he was talking about. "You didn't have to do that." She shook the ornament like a bell. "I was there once."

"Me too."

Setting the popcorn on the table, she stood. "Maybe our paths will cross again," she told the old man. "You never know."

Then she strode out of the café into the waiting room to catch the bus home. Her hand circled Graceland. In line for the bus, she glanced down at the bauble and burst out laughing. She felt like singing.

# South of Peculiar

---•◦•◦•---

Private First Class Thomas Creek was on his way home. On the Rez he was known to everybody as Tommy, but his gun truck crew in Iraq had christened him Tom-Tom and the name had stuck. It was etched into him permanently now, like his new tattoo.

Behind reflective sunglasses the young soldier's russet eyes were dimmed by a hangover. He was nineteen years old, with no beard to speak of, a fact the guys in his unit never let him forget. Against his ruddy face and hands, the stippled desert camo looked like worn pajamas. Under his sleeve his left bicep throbbed. The new tat was still so red and raised it was hard to make out the face engraved in the flesh, or the words and numbers written below it.

Tom-Tom sat with his back to the dark end of the bus station. Vending machines shared wall space with homeless men on soiled bedrolls. The original station had been built under city streets so that when the traffic rolled over the roof, the entire building shuddered and boomed like distant artillery fire.

As was his habit, Tom-Tom scanned his environment for risks. At twenty-three hundred hours, the Indianapolis station was way too quiet. The waiting room spilled over with mute, restless bodies. A barefoot white woman slumped in a chair, nodded out, her arms floating above her head like tentacles underwater. Her t-shirt read: *Good girls go to Heaven. Bad girls go everywhere.* Across from her, a grizzled black man slept, hunched over his knees, using them as a pillow. On the floor near the loading gates, a migrant family clustered on their coats, their belongings in cardboard boxes, the parents clutching their tickets and their children.

Tom-Tom had been traveling forty-eight hours, long flights over continents and oceans. The stewed green of the Midwest summer had ambushed his senses, overwhelming the vast colorless expanses he'd known for the past year-and-a-half. Tall, leaf-crowned trees hemmed in the rolling prairie with a calm insistence he did not trust. His right knee bounced like a jackhammer. Last night had been spent here in Indianapolis, drinking with a buddy from his brigade. Now he was on his own, waiting for the bus to Kansas City. From there, he would make a connection to Nevada, Missouri where his aunt and uncle lived, and they would drive him to his folks on the reservation in Oklahoma.

Without his Kevlar or M-16 in his hands, Tom-Tom felt naked. The sensation of weightlessness could go from pleasant to painful in a heartbeat and he had no control over what would bring the anxiety on. *Road withdrawal,* the army doc had called it. The only medicine Tom-Tom had found for it was running ridiculously long distances. He'd have run all the way home from Iraq if they'd let him.

He hated to admit it, but he missed the war. Not the blistering heat, or all the army bullshit, or the daily harangue from his teammates on convoy patrol: *Let's sacrifice the Injun!* No, what he missed was the adrenaline rush of forty, fifty, sixty supply trucks hurling down a rutted highway at sixty, seventy, eighty miles an hour, the pumped-up alertness of watching for *Ali Baba,* and the sheer exhilaration of being that stupid and alive.

*Know what I mean, Jellybean?*

Behind the mirrored shades Tom-Tom surveyed the room again. The only discernible movement came from a large family of Hutterites occupying a corner of the waiting area. Above them, a huge flat-screen

TV silently broadcasted CNN. Their skin was so alabaster, it was almost clear. Short dark bangs framed the men's pale foreheads. They wore flat-brimmed black hats and handmade pants, shirts, suspenders. The women had on full-length cotton dresses that showed their figures and scalloped bonnets that hid their faces. The children were miniature versions of the adults, down to their laughs and yawns. Like time travelers from another age, they looked as if they were trying to get back to their century by bus.

An older woman from their group was walking a mewling newborn around the waiting room. Her pastel cap had slipped from her head, revealing pewter-grey braids, cheeks like plums, and a clear blue gaze. Beside the rundown concession stand with its misspelled menu, she looked almost surreal. Her clean-scrubbed face made Tom-Tom uneasy. Passing his chair, she gave the young soldier a fleeting but radiant smile.

Like a switch thrown accidentally, adrenaline flooded Tom-Tom's body. His heart banged on his chest, his eyesight sharpened, his breathing picked up. Under fire these responses had kept him alive, but here there was nowhere to put this inconvenient outpour of energy, no circumstances dire enough to absorb the knee-jerk reactions to danger, real or misconstrued. The urge to bolt was coursing through Tom-Tom's legs with a thousand poisonous pinpricks, drawing up his hamstrings, flexing his feet. The ballooning panic swelled into his chest, arching his neck, and shooting out through his arms, splaying his fingers like flowers forced to bloom out-of-season.

Tom-Tom pushed his boots into the floor to keep himself in the chair. If this was his response to a stranger's unexpected smile, what would happen when he saw his aunt and uncle, Jellybean's mother and father, in Nevada? Or hugged their grandmother on the Rez? Would he ever be just Tommy again?

A woman's voice came on the intercom, stern as a commanding officer: "Okay. Listen up. This is your first and final call for Schedule 1934 to St. Louis. Making stops in Terre Haute, Effingham, Vandalia, and St. Louis. With connections for Kansas City, Little Rock, Denver, and all points west. Gate Number 3. All aboard."

At that the waiting room came alive. Bodies jolted awake, stretched, and pivoted upwards. The underwater woman surfaced and stood. Behind her, Gate 3 had become a checkpoint, complete with locked doors and impatient travelers stomping up against them.

Tom-Tom snapped to attention and sprinted for the line. His legs were trembling, he was panting for no reason. If it weren't for the people waiting for him on the Rez, he was tempted to keep on running.

*Know what I mean, Jellybean?*

\* \* \*

"Jesus died. Jesus died. What can you do? What can you do?"

It was still dark outside when Tom-Tom made his last connection in Kansas City. The furtive refrain bombarded him as he boarded the crowded bus.

"Jesus died. Jesus died. What can you do? What can you do?"

The young soldier made his way past blankets spread like army tents over snoring bodies. Instinctively he sought the source of the numbing repetition. There, by a window on his left, sat a husky white male, hair wispy, disheveled, and partially covered by a spidery hand, muttering to himself over and over, "Jesus died. Jesus died. What can you do? What can you do?"

"You can shut the fuck up," another man's voice piped up, further back.

"Language," the driver called out from his cab in the front. The word floated over Tom-Tom's head as if suspended in a helium bubble, too lightly put to have much weight.

The repeater continued. "Jesus died. Jesus died. What can you do? What can you do?"

The bus edged backwards out of its lane. Tom-Tom bee-lined for the coveted last seat but he was too late. A woman with short-cropped platinum hair had laid claim to all three spaces. She was sitting by the window, the other two seats barricaded with bright shopping bags that shone even in the dark. Dressed like a man in a beige golf-jacket and matching pants, every inch of the woman jangled with palsy, as if each separate nerve ending hung from its own microscopic Slinky. She looked as though, at any moment, she might shake herself apart.

Her eyes were a murky blue, the shadows of icebergs. Tom-Tom knew those eyes. The dark-eyed *hajji* women in Iraq had the same message in theirs: *This is mine.* Every day they crouched by the highway with their children, staring out of their long black *abayas,* begging for food and water from the American soldiers. His team leader would send Tom-Tom to chase them away, even though they all knew the women would return, like insistent mirages, before the gun trucks were forty yards down the road.

"Jesus died. Jesus died. What can you do? What can you do?"

Tom-Tom dropped into the empty aisle seat in front of the jangling woman. The anxiety was rising again. He slammed his feet into the floor to try and anchor them there. Beside him a rangy white guy in a torn down-jacket was sleeping, his long limbs plastered to the glass pane as if by a blast of wind. A white garbage bag peeked out from under his seat. Tom-Tom drew a sharp breath. *Ali Baba* hid IEDs in plastic bags just like that. He exhaled. This one probably held the guy's toothbrush and a pair of dirty mismatched socks.

"Jesus died. Jesus died. What can you do? What can you do?"

"You believe that motherfucker?" Tom-Tom's neighbor had spoken. He pushed his arms away from the window and stretched them above his head. His fingers were upside-down spiders doing push-ups on the overhead rack. "He's been saying that shit since Chicago," he told the rack.

Tom-Tom's feet tapped the floor. His knees shook. He removed his sunglasses and rubbed his eyes. They felt gritty. He tasted sand on his tongue.

"Jesus died. Jesus died. What can you do? What can you do?"

"Shit! I know what I'd do!" Tom-Tom's neighbor declared. He bent over the garbage bag, spreading its mouth like a fish to show Tom-Tom the pistol nestled in among his clean, folded underwear and socks.

Tom-Tom's fists unclenched. "Is that thing loaded?" The gun was a .45 caliber revolver, much like the one he and Jellybean had learned to shoot cans with on the Rez.

The guy snickered. "What do you think? Sometimes the mercy just runs out, you know what I'm saying, man?"

He slapped Tom-Tom on the arm with the back of his hand. Tom-Tom winced. Slowly, carefully, he rolled his sleeve up and over the new tattoo, until the cloth was bunched almost to his shoulder. He blew on the smarting skin. His neighbor ducked his head to peer at the wound. It was a festering blotch but here and there, like pieces of a puzzle, Tom-Tom could decipher a bright eye, the inky cleft of the chin.

"Know who gives the best tat?" he asked, without waiting for an answer. "*Hajji* in Iraq."

The guy squinted at the soldier's arm. "Don't look like shit to me."

"That's my cousin," Tom-Tom explained. "Jellybean. He signed up 'cause of me. Stupid fuck. Got himself blown up."

His neighbor's eyes showed bloodstained whites. "No shit?"

"No shit. Fucking fool-around. Just had to have that helmet." Tom-Tom flung his hands in the air. "*Kaboom.*"

He had been warned. Jellybean had been warned – and not just by Tom-Tom. They had been lucky, as far as luck went. They'd been able to stay together their whole time in theater. Side-by-side, they had endured these demeaning nicknames and the tantalizing fear. The helmet looked suspicious, sitting out in the sand by itself, the only object in the barren landscape for miles.

Jellybean was stubborn. He would prove them all wrong. If Tom-Tom hadn't seen him explode, there'd be little left to prove he had been there at all. Tom-Tom blew on his cousin's portrait.

*I had to bring something of you home, Jellybean.*

*   *   *

"Jesus died. Jesus died. What can you do? What can you do?"

The refrain lulled Tom-Tom into fitful dozing. He knew he was sleeping because he had begun to dream. A snake was hissing in his ear. Or was it a vulture? Scolding him – for what? He opened his eyes.

A quivering mask floated above him, spewing the words: "Thief! Satan! Dog of hell!"

Tom-Tom sat up. He was wide awake now. The jangling woman was leaning over his seatback, whispering into his ear in a high insistent trill. "Why do you steal from a poor woman? Why? Why? Thief! Satan! Dog of hell!"

There was no time to reply. From under the bus came a loud explosive *pop!* Tom-Tom sprang to his feet. The jangling woman fell back as if shot. The bus trembled and slowed.

"It seems we have a flat tire," the driver announced, as if he were telling them the time. The familiar flap-flap-flap of rubber was comforting to Tom-Tom. The road-weary supply-trucks he and his gun crew protected blew out tires daily, sometimes hourly. The *hajji* truck driver would automatically throw on his brakes, forcing all the vehicles behind him to scatter off the road. The trick was to avoid slamming into the disabled truck without hitting the beggars in the ditch. Jellybean was especially effective at these maneuvers. Every gun truck team wanted Jellybean for their driver. He, not Tom-Tom, was the true warrior.

The bus driver managed to get the hobbled vehicle off the highway. He rose from behind the wheel. A compact, hard-muscled black man, he had the measured bearing of someone who'd seen it all. Leaning an arm on the frame of the cab, he faced his passengers with a resigned smile.

"We are just south of Peculiar," he stated. "I'm going to step out and call for assistance." His eye fell on Tom-Tom in his camouflage, standing in the aisle. The driver tapped the brass name tag on his chest.

"Operation: Freedom," he informed Tom-Tom. "225th out of Illinois." He watched Tom-Tom shift from foot to foot, as if he were running in place. "You still playing in that sandbox?"

"I deploy to Afghanistan in September, sir," was Tom-Tom's panting reply.

The driver waved a hand toward the soldier. "I'm leaving this man in charge," he announced. Before Tom-Tom could protest, he tossed a "You children behave" over his shoulder and turned out the door.

Tom-Tom sat back down. He was shivering. He tried to catch his breath. He unrolled his sleeve to cover the tattoo. His uniform was wet with sweat. His pulse pounded in his head.

"Jesus died. Jesus died. What can you do? What can you do?" The repeater had picked up his pace and volume.

Tom-Tom's neighbor held his hands over his ears and kicked his feet. "Shut that motherfucker up! Shut him up!"

Tom-Tom did not move. Down in front an elderly black lady began rapping on a window. "My brother!" she called to the driver pacing on the shoulder, his cell phone mashed to his ear. "My brother!" she cried again, through the window. "You tell them folks to hurry now. Tell 'em there's colored folks on this bus and there'll be white folks in sheets coming out of the woods for us! My brother!" She rapped again. "You hurry now!"

Yelping laughter pinged through the bus. There was scattered clapping and whoops of approval. An old black man stood up, waving a red pillow in circles around his head like the blades of a helicopter. "My bro-ther, my bro-ther," he chanted amicably.

Tom-Tom watched a bag of chips arc across the aisle, followed by a fat bottle of soda. The soda missed the seat, hit the floor, and burst. Soda fizzed on the old man's jeans as he sashayed into the aisle.

"My bro-ther. My bro-ther."

"Jesus died. Jesus died. What can you do? What can you do?"

A pair of hands was pressing down on Tom-Tom's shoulders. There was a screeching in his ear: "Satan! Thief! Dog of hell!" The jangling woman was spitting curses at him again.

The old man wriggled up the aisle toward Tom-Tom, the soles of his sneakers dripping brown soda, the pillow twirling red above his head. "My bro-ther. My bro-ther."

A second bag of chips came whizzing across the bus. The old man dodged them expertly, then bending low as if under a limbo stick, avoided a pair of shoes making a similar trip.

"Satan! Thief! Dog of hell!"

The repeater stood, spreading his arms. "Jesus died. Jesus died. What can you do? What can you do?"

"I'll shut that motherfucker up!" Tom-Tom's neighbor roared. He dove into the garbage bag, pulled out the revolver and waved it in front of the soldier. The jangling woman shrieked and cowered. Tom-Tom pushed the guy's arm upward. *Bam!* The gun went off. Passengers screamed. The old man ducked into an empty seat, head first. Tom-Tom snatched the pistol from the guy's upraised hand. Jumping up, he pointed the barrel to the floor and cleared its chambers of bullets. He put the bullets in his pocket. The gun felt light in his hand.

The driver rushed onto the bus, shouting into his cell phone, "We have a situation! We have a situation!"

The hilarity inside had come to a shattered stop. Even the repeater had been silenced at last. "Happy now?" Tom-Tom asked his neighbor.

The guy stared dully up at the soldier. His lower jaw hung as if it had sprung its hinges. He made no response.

"It was an accident," the soldier explained to the driver, casting a thumb at his neighbor.

The driver inspected the damaged rack. The bullet had made a clean hole through the shelf, a cooler full of clothing, and the roof of the bus. He glared at Tom-Tom's neighbor. "You are in deep doo-doo, pal."

The neighbor scowled at Tom-Tom, then flipped over on his side and tied his long length into an angry knot. The driver placed a hand on each of Tom-Tom's upper arms and squeezed them hard. "God bless you, son."

Tom-Tom willed himself not to cringe. "Thank you, sir."

Above the scattered applause he heard the fast-approaching sirens. His tattoo burned from the grip of the driver's hand.

The jangling woman rose to her feet, pointing a palsied finger at Tom-Tom. "This man stole from me," she shrilled to the driver. "He is a thief!"

Tom-Tom's neighbor unknotted himself. "That's right! The motherfucker took my gun!"

"Jesus died. Jesus died. What can you do? What can you do?" The repeater's refrain had begun again, even as the sirens drowned him out.

A strobe of blue lights surrounded the bus. Squad car doors opened and slammed shut. The driver did an about-face. Two state troopers boarded the bus, their hands on their holsters. Their bodies were as wide as the aisle.

"Jesus died, Jesus died. What can you do? What can you do?"

"Thief!" the jangling woman hissed. "Satan! Dog of hell!"

"Motherfucker!" Tom-Tom's neighbor sneered at him.

The state troopers came up the aisle toward Tom-Tom, eyes narrowed. The soldier was still holding the gun. Tom-Tom felt his body dissolve. He could stop running now. He clasped a hand over the stinging tattoo.

*We're home, Jellybean. We're home.*

# Approaching Normal

---

End-to-end, her ticket was over eight feet long, each leg of her journey separated by the thinnest of perforations. State by state, the segments fell away, like the broken white lines under the wheels of the bus. She had come to dread the sound of her ticket being torn. Every rip was an audible reminder that she had failed again to find him.

She carried little else with her: a purse, an inflatable pillow, a jacket, and a small roller suitcase jammed with journals, flyers, photos, a laptop, an extra pair of walking shoes, and two changes of clothes. She stayed with friends and family wherever she could, in YWCAs, and the occasional hostel. Many nights were spent on the bus. The search had taken her to places she'd never been before, geographically or emotionally. It didn't matter so long as they were locations *he* had once inhabited. A city or town he had lived in or loved in or mentioned in passing – all became her destinations. Already her travels had taken her to two oceans, one border, and twenty-seven states.

Basically, it was a nightmare. There were no clues, no leads, no random sightings. A website in his name had been up on the Internet for two years now. Twice a month she scoured the patient databases of hospitals and psychiatric facilities. Ads had been placed and replaced in all the major newspapers, posters with his photograph passed out in police stations all over the map. Methodical and precise, she was charting a paper trail as dense and dendritic as a genealogy tree.

To make matters worse, he was a chameleon, a master of disguise. Every Halloween of their childhood he had bested her, his costumes always convincing, less about detail, more about attitude. It was possible he had dyed his hair, let grow it long or shaved it all off. He could be wearing funky glasses and sporting a full beard. She did not know what to do about that; he wasn't a criminal, he was just gone.

Arriving in a new city, she paced the streets, scanning every face for his. Once she followed a familiar nape of neck for blocks without success. Hearing his laugh in a mall, she trailed it through several stores, even after it turned out to belong to a teenage girl. He could be passing her on the sidewalk across the avenue or walking right behind her and she would never know. There were times she spun around for no reason, hoping to surprise him out of the air. People avoided her as if she was crazy and likely dangerous.

The only time she encountered him was in her dreams. Technically, they were nightmares. Though she'd begun to view them as opportunities to spend time together. The details were recorded in her journal:

*Friday 7.26.03. Buffalo. Saw M. again. He was younger, fresh-faced and healthy, a kid almost. I don't know where we were. A quaint street in some quaint town. He was carrying his dry cleaning over his shoulder. I called to him but he didn't answer. He went around a corner and I lost him again.*

*Wednesday 8.11.03. On the way to Chicago. M. and I are sitting in an outdoor café drinking coffee. It could be Paris for all I know. (Note: Shit. If he's left the country I'm screwed) He says something like 'Mom was a restless goddess' and then we start making out. Even in the dream I know that this is weird.*

*Monday 9.4.03. St. Paul. I get on a bus. Everyone looks like M. He's dressed as different people – women, children, even*

*an old Chinese man, they all have his face. I keep asking,*
*"Are you Michael? Are you Michael?" Each says yes and*
*then they turn into me. Yikes.*

At times it felt like she was pursuing a ghost. There was no way to know if he was alive; he was HIV-positive when he vanished. She haunted graveyards, looking for his name. Finding him among the dead would be a bittersweet relief, if only to put to rest the unthinkable: that he was suffering and she was not there to comfort him.

Other times it felt as if *she* was the ghost. Her life had winnowed down to this one pursuit. Their apartment, the cars and a potential new boyfriend had all been sacrificed to the search for her brother. Her job as a tax accountant had gone the same way, leaving her to plow blindly through the cash-out on her 401K. Her existence was being held hostage to the inexhaustible need to know where Michael was and why he had left her.

His photo was glued to the inside cover of her journal. It was her habit now to visit with him whenever she got on a new bus taking her somewhere else. Today's destination was St. Louis. So far as she knew, her brother had never been there, but she could remember him talking about wanting to climb its famous arch.

Michael loved the Mississippi River and every word ever written by Tennessee Williams. He had played Tom in *The Glass Menagerie,* in what he called an "off-off-off-off Broadway" theater. That meant New Jersey. She had seen it three times. This was just months before Michael evaporated. Maybe – like Tom's wandering father in the play – her brother had "fallen in love with long distance." Unfortunately, she had not.

Looking at his picture was like looking in the mirror; they were so much alike, they could have been twins born fourteen months apart. Their bond was cemented by their mother's appetite for marriage. It seemed she preferred *getting* married to *being* married. She was constantly leaving them with some reluctant relative.

"Take care of Mikey," she'd say to her daughter, with an airy wave, showing up weeks later, new husband in tow. At one point she accumulated four in three years, discarding them like jokers in a losing game of hearts.

It had always been just the two of them, really. Until now. Michael's abandonment cut as deep as an amputation. He was not there, but she could still feel him and it hurt. True amputees call that *phantom pain*. That was Michael now, elusive as a phantom and just as cruel.

*   *   *

*Thursday 9.22.03. Approaching Normal (if there is such a thing anymore) IL. A strange dream. No images. Only my voice calling into the blackness: Mikey, Mikey. Over and over. Finally he replies. One word: Sad.*

"May I sit here?"

The cultured accent had a musical cadence. She glanced up from her journal. Her first impression was of skin so black it was blue, the second of the man's extraordinary height, accentuated by a full-length caftan of brilliant greens and reds traced with ivory and gold.

Nodding, she buried her head in the notebook. She wanted to stay with her dream, to maintain her tenuous grasp on Michael's voice. His message had remained on their answering machine for months. It had taken all her courage and a bottle of chardonnay to erase it. The thought that he could fade from her memory was more horrifying to her than the possibility that she might one day forget herself.

The man folded easily into the seat next to her. The robe gave him the appearance of having no bones. His knees poked into the seatback in front of him, an elbow rested without apology against hers. His wrists were spangled with copper bands, beaded bracelets, a Rolex.

The man's presence disrupted her hold on Michael's echo. And any lingering whisper was soon blasted away by the bus driver's rat-tat-tat announcements. Compared to the giant sitting next to her, the driver was a burly, non-descript black man, standing at the front of the bus, arms folded, legs apart. Like a drill sergeant facing a platoon of captive recruits, he barked through a standard litany of No's: No alcohol. No illegal drugs. No weapons. No foul language. No excessive noise from cell phones or CD players. Each prohibition was punctuated by an emphatic "You got that?"

"And no shouting at me down the aisle," he shouted. "You got that? You got a problem with the temperature, or your neighbor, you get up, you come down here, you let me know, you got that? Do not yell at me from your seat. Because that would be like committing suicide. Passenger suicide. Because I will put you off this bus, you got that?"

He paused, as if expecting them to shout back in unison, "Yes! Sir!" Instead he was greeted by a stunned silence.

"Good!" he hammered. "Now sit back, relax, and enjoy the ride. You got that?" Laughing manically, he jumped into the driver's seat. The horn sounded four times and the bus jerked to a start.

"He appears overwrought," the man beside her opined mildly.

She guffawed. "You got that? He's insane. They all are. You'd have to be."

"You have traveled on many buses." It was a simple statement of fact.

The bus maneuvered out of the Bloomington station. She closed the journal. "Yeah, I'm what's laughingly known as a free spirit."

He tilted his head, a large curious bird of paradise. "This is your vocation."

"It's no vacation, I can tell you that." She took a water bottle from her purse. "I like your dress," she commented, changing the subject.

The man's laugh was high and silly, revealing capped white teeth. She gulped some water. "Where you from?" she asked him.

"A little country in West Africa you have never heard of. Burkina Faso."

"You're right, I haven't. You probably never heard of where I'm from either."

"You are from *here.*" His hands made a grand gesture in the air.

"Let me ask you something." She replaced the cap on the bottle. "What does your country think of my country?"

He smiled sagely. "There are governments and there are people."

"Yeah. Tell that to a terrorist." She unscrewed the cap again. "So, what do you do?" She took another sip of water.

"I am a salesman for Wal-Mart."

Out sputtered the water. "Sorry." She wiped her chin with her hand. "Didn't take you for the Wal-Mart type."

"Shea butter."

"Excuse me?"

"A product of my country. Good for the skin. Good for blemishes and age spots." He tapped her cheek below her right eye. "Good for eyes that cry." His expression conveyed intolerable kindness.

"Did I say you could touch me?" she asked, and that put an end to the conversation.

\* \* \*

She would not allow herself to talk about Michael on the bus, any more than she would voluntarily offer her name. It was too demanding to have to explain their situation yet again and deal with yet another stranger's pity. On the bus her brother's defection stayed sealed up inside her, enlarged by the reticence to let it out. The bus had become an unlikely sanctuary, a moveable limbo between the agonizing realities of stopping and seeking, a temporary respite from the endless but necessary questions from the police and the free-floating barrage of unwanted opinions about where he might be and what she could do about it.

Off the bus she felt porous, a leaking sieve. Pieces of Michael drained out of her each time she had to recount their story. But their plight never failed to summon an earnest response. Helping her find her brother was an opportunity for others to heal what was still, two years later, an infected national wound.

Michael was temping on the 63$^{rd}$ floor of the North Tower when the first plane hit. She was sitting a mile away in a Cuban café in Jersey City where they shared the apartment, drinking *café con leche* and trying to wake up. A woman burst in. Smoke was pouring from the World Trade Center, she announced. She spoke in Spanish but there was no mistaking the news. They had all rushed out to the street.

The twin towers loomed above the southern end of Manhattan, the morning sun casting their gargantuan shadow over the mouth of the Hudson River and the piers spiking out from the Jersey shore. The top half of the North Tower was hidden in thick black smoke. The people around her were already on their cell phones. She fumbled with hers, speed-dialing Michael's number. Her eyes lifted just in time to see the second plane – black as a shark in the shadow of the skyscraper – hurl itself with ferocious intention at the South Tower. A silent orange fireball ballooned from the building. She didn't stay to see what happened next but hurried back home in case Michael should call her there.

He didn't call. She couldn't get him on her phone. She was certain he was dead and that she and everyone else in Jersey City were going to die, too. A plane would fly into the toxic chemical vats that dotted the New Jersey landscape like witches' cauldrons and they would all choke a painful death. She watched the TV and tried to figure out how to suffocate the dog, so he wouldn't have to watch her die, or suffer himself. The towers fell. The Pentagon was hit. A fourth plane went down in Pennsylvania. She and the dog were still alive – but no Michael. All afternoon ambulance sirens clanged through Jersey City, triaging victims to local hospitals.

Finally, at three pm he called. He was fine, he assured her, freaked out but okay. "I'm going back to see what I can do," he informed her.

"Come home," she insisted. "I'm scared."

"Sissy, you will be all right."

That was the last thing he said before he hung up. At six pm the sirens stopped. There were no more victims to rescue. Michael did not come home that night or the following night or for countless nights after. She contacted everyone they knew, even their dying cousin in Oregon. No one had seen or heard from him. His name was posted on a 9/11 web site for missing persons. She wrote in to tell them that he was in touch with her after the tragedy, that he had survived it. But when they followed up to ask how he was doing, she didn't answer back.

Shock could have altered him down to his cells. After all, she was different now, too. The attack's effects had lasted weeks, months; Michael's desertion kept the details alive. Anything could remind her of that day: steam rising from a bowl of soup; a towel falling from its rack; a turd in the toilet in the shape of the lethal plane. Invisible fault lines in her psyche had been deepened by the shattered illusion of safety. There was a reason she was riding this bus; she would never get on a plane again. The terrorists had won that one, too.

The not-knowing – that was what made his absence so excruciating. Two days after the attack she had volunteered for the phone bank at St. Francis Hospital in Jersey City, answering calls from people searching for lost loved ones. Each volunteer was given a long list of injured victims recovering in Jersey hospitals. Michael's name was not among them.

She spoke to a man with an Indian accent: "Have you seen my wife? She worked on the 102nd floor? She was six months pregnant." A young Italian woman who sobbed: "Do you have my husband there? Please. He was a firefighter." Of the hundreds of calls she fielded that day, she was only able to reunite one family. The disaster worker who organized the phone banks told her, "The people whose family died in those planes? They're lucky. They know their loved ones are dead."

\* \* \*

*Thursday 9.22.03. Leaving Springfield IL. (Dreamt beside an African Paul Bunyan in a muu-muu) I'm looking for M. in a big old house. I don't recognize it. I go up the stairs and I'm sure I've hit the attic but there's always a new floor. The place just keeps growing. I'm so high off the ground I feel dizzy and then I fall. I think, okay, I'm going to die. I don't seem to mind much. The ground rushes toward me. It turns out to be water and I wake up in a puddle of drool. Lovely.*

Between Springfield and St. Louis, the bus stopped at a rural grocery off the interstate. She got out and bought a Mound's bar, Michael's favorite. The afternoon sun backlit the trees, tingeing the leaves with red and yellow fire. Autumn would never fail to bring back that Tuesday: the shimmering blue September sky, the silver triangular jetfighters streaking over Manhattan, the monstrous pillars of smoke and ash drifting out to sea.

It was possible she would never learn how Michael escaped the collapsing towers. Or what he did after he hung up. Had he gone back into the wreckage? Buildings were still falling. He might have died at Ground Zero that day, his body crushed, never to be identified. Or did he bolt that same afternoon, walking out of the city and out of her life, into a new life all his own? That possibility could still enrage her. What right did he have to abandon her at the moment they needed each other most? Hadn't she always been there for him?

He had to be traumatized; that was the only plausible explanation. His confusion had caused him to lose his mind. Surely forgetfulness would be an effective balm. But what if he knew exactly what he was doing? She had asked herself this question so many times. She thought she'd go mad unless she found an answer. Had Michael made a conscious, rational decision to leave her? The thought was unbearable. Only insanity could justify such cold-heartedness.

She wandered around to the back of the store. Crows were feeding on food scraps spilling from a dumpster. Sitting on the curb of the graveled lot was a painfully thin, young, white man holding up an illegible cardboard sign. A Styrofoam cup sat at his feet. The way his knees bent, the angle at which they turned inward, gave him a familiar knock-kneed vulnerability. His forearms were traced with a blue vein that curved along the muscle much like hers. Holding her breath, she drew closer. The crows skittered off their scraps. Scrawled on the sign were the words: *HIV-positive. Homeless. I need help.*

"M-Michael?" She could barely get his name out.

The panhandler lifted red eyes. The irises were a pale washed-out blue, not at all like her brother's chestnut brown.

"I'm sorry." She opened her purse for some change. "I thought you were someone else."

"I wish I was." He sounded drunk.

Stuffing ten-dollars into his cup, she stumbled away. The crows flapped up to the rim of the dumpster, scolding. Her hands flew to her mouth; her chest rose and fell in silent hiccoughs. She leaned against the cinderblock wall and gave in to months of pent-up grief.

After a moment a large hand cupped her shoulder. The African stood beside her, colorful and mute. She dragged a sleeve across her face and tried to make light of her embarrassing display of emotion.

"I'm going to need some of that Shea butter," she gulped.

He squinted at the beggar's sign. "In my country we have many such people. Very bad sickness. That is why I am here. To make money. To send to my father. My sister. So they can buy medicine."

His story, and the lightness with which he told it, had a soothing effect. She caught her breath. "Do you ever go back?"

He swung his huge head. "It is hard for me. No one knows who I am anymore."

"But still, you dress like this?"

"I do not wish to disappoint my customers." Smiling, he took her arm. "Come. The bus driver is very strict."

They boarded and took their seats. This time she did not move her elbow away. She pretended to sleep but as always she was thinking about Michael, imagining for the first time who he might be without her. She was struck by a sudden new terror: the fear of her own blindness. Was there something she had missed? A subtle sign, an unspoken signal, that he was unhappy with the way things were between them? Was he already inching toward the door when the attacks blew it open and covered his tracks?

In her mind Michael would always be a child. He couldn't balance his checkbook or keep track of his medications. He liked to joke that his personal best with boyfriends was under seventy-two hours. If she held him too close, it was because he needed it. How could he navigate life without her?

*Sissy, you will be all right.*

What did he mean by that? And why even bother to call? It would have been far kinder to let her believe he was dead. At least then she could grieve and be done with it. The idea he might be blaming her for their separation was too painful to carry alone or in silence.

"I'm looking for someone," she blurted aloud.

The African twisted his body toward her, as if he had been waiting for her to confess. His dark eyes pounced. "Perhaps *I* am that someone."

She ignored his implication. "No. You don't get it. I'm chasing him and I don't even know who he is."

"You are chasing a fantasy."

"No! I don't know! I don't know anything anymore."

He nodded. "A good place to start. Perhaps when this someone wants to be found, *he* will find *you*."

"What are you saying? I should just give up?"

"No. You do not give up. You wait."

\* \* \*

*9.26.03. St. Louis. I'm fishing on a river. The Mississippi? Bloated dead dogs float on the water. I snag one by mistake and reel it in. There is something written on its tongue (Note: I think we saw this in an X-rated Japanese movie once). The message is in a language I can't read.*

Her time in St. Louis proved futile. The usual tasks were accomplished: flyers were delivered, ads placed, the paper trail expanded and entered on the laptop. Wandering the streets, peering into faces, for the first time she checked the homeless shelters and hospital emergency rooms.

One afternoon was spent with the African. His name, as it turned out, was Zanga. She and Zanga took a pleasant riverboat ride up and down the Mississippi. She had forgotten what it was like to play at being normal, to have no driven purpose for a few aimless hours. Zanga was as kind as ever and increasingly persistent. He wanted her to come with him to Burkina Faso. She would give him the strength to go back and she, in turn, would learn what real suffering was. She resisted; she was on a mission here with miles still to go. On parting, Zanga gave her his card, a month's supply of Shea butter, and the solemn declaration that he would be patient.

She was running out of destinations, of locations that Michael had traveled to, if only in his imagination. That left the rest of the country, not to mention the world. After St. Louis she already had booked a ticket to Colorado because Michael liked to ski. From Denver she was scheduled to go to Seattle, where five years ago he spent a season with a repertory company there. Purchasing her ticket in advance gave her something tangible to hold on to. It lent her the sense, false or not, that she knew what she was doing. A ticket-in-hand was her only safety net in this choreographed free fall.

While still in St. Louis, she received an email from a man in Ohio. He had met a fellow who fit the description she had posted with the local police. They worked at the sock mill together. The man had gotten a name and number for her.

It took her an hour to summon the nerve. When she finally dialed the number for a Stanley Lambert, the voice that answered was not Michael's. Unless he had taken to disguising his.

"Michael?" she quavered into the phone.

"I'm sorry, who did you want?" the alleged Mr. Lambert asked.

"Wrong number," she stated, and put down the receiver.

On her last day in St. Louis, she climbed the thousand steps to the top of the Gateway Arch. The impressively-odd metal structure was built to celebrate the opening of the American West there beyond the Mississippi. Below the observation windows, the river flowed north and south, disappearing into low circular horizons. The flatlands made flatter by a cloudless, blue-domed sky. She found herself wondering what it would be like to jump from this height.

Exhaustion was dismantling her resolve. She was weary of the constant movement, the second-guessing, the endless disappointments. The absurdity of her task was becoming harder to deny. She was trying to make order where there was none. For a long time hope had propelled her forward; now that was dwindling, too, along with her determination. Death was an unknown, but then so was life. What a welcome relief it would be to let go of everything she could not make right.

Gazing at a bridge that spanned the wide water, she suddenly recalled something Michael had said about the Arch: how its curving shape reminded him of a white rainbow with all the separate hues of the spectrum collected into one dazzling reality. She had teased him then, called him ridiculous. How could a rainbow be white? Now she missed his foolishness so much.

And what if death was just that, a merger of color? What if he had gone away to die peaceably, like a dog in the woods? Perhaps he had wanted to spare her his suffering; that thought had never occurred to her before. If only she believed in an afterlife, where they might one day meet. Was there a heaven for deserters? Suicide seemed like a simple escape, but suppose she was wrong about that, too? It was not in her nature to give up, any more than it was to wait.

\* \* \*

*10.06.03. Night before leaving St. Louis. I'm with M. We're knocking on the door of our former landlord. Somehow we get inside and stuff our pockets with his sterling. Then we're on the street in front of the Cuban café. The Towers are burning behind us. M. is giving away his silverware. I'm so angry with him I'm stamping my feet. I stamp and stamp and get smaller and smaller until I (literally) drop out of the dream. Then I'm sailing on my back through a*

*perfect cloud-strewn sky, cartoon-like, straight out of the*
*Simpsons. A winged horse catches me – what do you call it?*
*A Pegasus. Good God, whose dream is this?*

The bus to Denver was idling in the St. Louis station. She had gotten there hours early to insure a window seat. Once on board, the dream of the night before was duly noted in her journal. She was communing with Michael's likeness when a woman came and sank down beside her, clutching an aromatic paper bag from Chik-fil-A.

"I just left my husband," her new seatmate announced.

She turned and peered at the woman. She was small and bony with caramel-colored skin. An orange fleece hat covered her head to just above her eyebrows.

"Only took me fifteen years," she went on. She spoke with unnerving calm. Pulling off the cap, she took a comb from her coat pocket and dragged it through stiff, overhanging bangs.

"I'm going to Denver," she explained. "Got me a sister there. If she hadn't moved." She pocketed the comb and held out a calloused hand. "I'm Florence by the way."

"Cecelia," the other woman replied, pumping Florence's fingers without enthusiasm.

"That's a pretty name."

Florence opened the bag and took out the still-hot sandwich. "Things I've been through, hon." She arranged the lettuce between the slices of bun. "You don't want to know."

She was going to tell her anyway. It was a long story and an awful one, told in that same untroubled manner, a tale of broken bones, knives and guns, hospitalizations, miscarriages and three live births. Her kids were older now. Florence had sent them to live with her mother in Urbana until her life got settled somewhere else.

At one point Cecelia interrupted to ask the obvious. "Why did you stay?"

"Stupid," Florence admitted, with no remorse. "Scared. What he'd do to me. This isn't the first time I tried to leave. Uh-uh. He always finds me out." She pursed her lips. "Not this time. No mam. I am not going back."

The highway rolled through Missouri and evened out in Kansas. Florence talked into the night. At last she fell asleep, her bare head lolling on Cecelia's shoulder.

Florence's weight kept Cecelia awake. She dared not move and disturb her. Beyond the window, farmhouses and trailers were colorless and formless under the stars. In the half-light Florence's skin was mottled with round gray scars, like fingerprints pressed into the flesh. She was running away, just as Michael had done. Before 9/11, Cecelia could never understand how people in war-torn countries went on. That day she learned: you just do. You walk the dog, you empty the trash, every act drenched in sorrow and dread. But you could only endure so much and then you snapped. The need to find her brother was being fueled by an impulse deeper and more ordinary than a broken heart. If she never found him, if she never made peace with his departure, one way or another the lack of closure would kill her.

Five months after Michael's disappearance, the dog had been diagnosed with cancer of the snout. In the weeks following the attacks, the air over Jersey City was permeated by the toxic innards of thousands of pulverized computers. As far as she was concerned, the dog had died from breathing in asbestos particles blown west into New Jersey. He had been a victim of that day, too. If she were to die of uncertainty, the terrorists could claim another. They would win them all.

And maybe they already had. The country was fighting senseless wars in Afghanistan and Iraq. Airlines might go bankrupt because cowards like her were afraid to fly. The altered Manhattan skyline had been a fresh blow every morning. It had not been as difficult to leave Jersey City as she expected. She was running, too. All this meticulous effort was just a blind insistence on life being the way she required it to be. For two years her search had served as a distraction. She was overbearing, she admitted it; she had sought to control Michael's every move. Maybe she *had* pushed him out the door. In any event, he had found the strength to go. And he had assumed, rightly or wrongly, that she would find the courage to survive without him.

She leaned her cheek against Florence's hair. The turn of the wheels lulled her to sleep.

\* \* \*

At dawn she jumped awake. She and Florence were nose-to-nose now, their faces inches apart. Their eyes opened at the same moment.

"Good morning, Cecelia."

It was strange to hear her name spoken aloud on the bus. Florence stretched like a cat. "I need to call my daughter."

The bus stopped at a travel plaza in western Kansas. In the drab diner Cecelia purchased a cup of bad coffee and watched Florence fill up the payphone with coins. When Florence began to talk, Cecelia walked back to the bus. At this hour many of the passengers were still sleeping, their bodies contorted to fit the seats. Cecelia took hers. Her mind was jangled from shreds of dreams and lack of sleep.

After a while Florence came back on. She sat heavily, her hands clasped so tightly the knuckles were pink. "My daughter said he called there," she reported, without expression. "Told them kids he knew I was going to my sister and he was coming after me."

She rocked in her seat. "What am I going to do?"

Cecelia tried to think how she could help her. She doubted Florence would accept money but what else did she have? Her cell phone? A pair of walking shoes? Some Shea butter? There *was* her ticket to Seattle, only that was impossible. She needed it and besides, her name was on it.

"What am I going to do?" Florence repeated. "I am a dead woman."

Cecelia heard a new note of resignation in Florence's voice. Had there been some stranger there to comfort Michael when he fled? Was there someone to keep him on track when doubt and fear overtook him?

She squeezed Florence's fingers the way she had Michael's for decades. "Florence," she asserted. "You will be all right."

Hearing herself say those words, it struck her then that maybe her brother had called her because he didn't want terror to win either. Maybe he had called because he loved her.

Reaching into her purse, she found her ticket to Seattle and held it out to Florence. "I want you to have this."

Florence blinked. "What is it?"

Cecelia pushed the folded pages into Florence's hand. "I hear Washington State is beautiful this time of year."

"What?" Florence stared at the ticket." No, no." She tried to give it back. "I can't have that, that's yours."

Cecelia hid her hands. "Take it. Complimentary Shea butter included."

Florence's eyes widened. She regarded the ticket with disbelief. "It says two weeks from now."

"We'll change it in Denver."

"It's got your name on it."

"No one will notice unless you misbehave. Look at it this way: your husband will never be able to trace you."

Florence took a ragged breath. "What about you?"

"What about me? I'll get another, I'll take a plane. I'll think of something."

At the Denver bus station, Florence hid in the ladies' room while Cecelia went to the ticket counter to exchange her ticket for the next bus to Seattle. It left in less than an hour.

On the loading dock Florence held onto her. "I won't ever forget you, Cecelia," she whispered.

Cecelia waved until Florence's bus had rounded the corner. Then she went back inside the station. She bought an egg salad sandwich and sat at a café table next to the video games. A group of teenage boys surrounded a booth. The tallest boy swung his hair when he laughed, much the way Michael used to do. She took a bite of her sandwich, opened her journal, and wrote:

> 10.08.03 On the bus to Denver. I'm a waitress in a diner somewhere. I'm actually wearing this geeky little red-and-white uniform. (Note: I've never done this before, not even in real life). No one seems to care that I don't know what I'm doing. I pick up a tip at a table and then I realize the person I've been serving is me. I look around but I'm already gone. I run out the door. Wait, I yell. I run into the street. Wait. Wait. Wait. Then I wake up next to Florence.

She closed the notebook and packed it away in her suitcase. The bag bumped behind her, wheels grating on broken tiles as she walked out onto the street. It was late morning. The sidewalk was dark in the shade of downtown. High up, a jet flew across the band of blue between the skyscrapers, a pinpoint of silver leaving in its wake a single white contrail.

# The Nashville Institute of Beauty and Poise

Okay, she was beautiful, any fool could see that. Everywhere she went, men's eyes – women's too – stuck to her like Krazy Glue. It didn't faze her anymore. She was used to it. It was her fate.

Only the bus driver was blind to her charms. The guy had a wig on that looked like it'd been machine-washed and rode over by a tractor. He made her put out her last cigarette before she was even done with it. And his second mistake was giving her shit about Snuggles.

"No pets," he smirked, taking her ticket.

She stuck out her bottom lip. "He's my bodyguard." Like she was going anywhere without the pink stuffed poodle her ex had won for her at the Little River County fair.

The driver grunted. "Where's his ticket?"

"Ha ha. You're funny."

He smirked. His rug slid forward like a tipped cap. "Change in Texarkana for Nashville, gorgeous."

She snatched the ticket and climbed on board. Heads turned like flowers to the sun as she came down the aisle. Not one of them would've guessed she'd never been on a bus before. Hell, she'd never been out of Umpire before.

She had two choice seats picked out for herself when this grease ball came out of nowhere and oozed in beside her. Marcos-or-Mayonnaise or whatever the fuck his name was. She wedged Snuggles between them.

Mayo giggled. He pawed the dog. "Nice *perro*." Even his accent dripped. "Is good luck, *sí*?"

She snorted. "I don't need luck, see?"

What she did need was a clean smile. Digging in her purse for a strip of tooth whitener, she stuck it on her front teeth like a Band-Aid. She had to look perfect, not like some hayseed that just spent eleven hours on a bus next to some Mexican Romeo. Plucking up Snuggles, she shoved him against the window, put her cheek to his velvety fur and closed her eyes.

Next thing she knew, a hand was creeping up her thigh. She smacked it away. "Okay, this is fucked up."

Mayo laughed with delight. She squinted out the window. "Where are we?"

He grinned like a possum. "Heaven?"

She lifted her top lip. "How are my teeth?"

"Beautiful."

"No! I mean, are they white?"

The strip came off with a yank and went on the floor. She pulled a cracked mirror from her jeans pocket. She obviously liked what she saw in it: white powdery skin, stiff golden hair curled to her shoulders, dark blue eyes that were caked with mascara, a pug nose that was only slightly pig-like. She parted her lips the way she'd seen the models do on TV. Her lips were full and pink and –

"Shit."

Her teeth were hopeless. A dingy yellow like that first pee after a night of slugging tequila and Mountain Dew. She'd been drinking coffee and smoking cigarettes, not to mention weed, since she was ten.

She tore through her purse. Mayo leaned in. "Tell me you do not have a husband."

"Tell me I got more whiteners."

She found the box. Empty. "God damn it!" It went on the floor, too. Mayo laughed again. He clearly found her adorable.

"What are you lookin' at?" she demanded. She was afraid he might drool on her. "Hey!" she shouted before Mayo could reply. "I just broke up with my boyfriend, okay? And he's better lookin' than you'll ever be."

Mayo put his hands together with his elbows out. He grinned and pumped his fists twice beside each ear. She knew where he was going with that.

"Forget it, bozo," she snarled. "Listen. We got up this mornin' and my ex says to me, 'Okay, beautiful girl, you're free. Go get 'em.' Because hey, you know? Look at this."

She pulled a piece of paper from her bra. Mayo practically swooned. "I am looking," he murmured.

"Shut up, loser."

She held up the ad between his eyes and her tits. The box around it was decorated with teeny-weeny stars she'd drawn in blue ink. The print was smeared with swipes of yellow magic marker. It didn't matter. She knew every word by heart:

> *Do people tell you you're beautiful?*
> *That you deserve love, success, riches, and fame?*

"Come on!" she yelled. "Is that me or what?"

*The Nashville Institute of Beauty and Poise*

"Po-easy," she pronounced it. "Whatever." She didn't know what it meant.

*Can turn these questions into answers.*
*For only six hundred and ninety-nine dollars*
*You will receive one week of instruction*
*In make-up, hair, posture, and runway demeanor.*

She pressed the page to her boobs. "Tell me that isn't so awesome." There were actual tears in her eyes. "Only one thing sucks." She pointed to the hateful words: *No smokers please.*

Fuck!" she hollered. "What do they want from me? Do you know?"

Mayo shook his head. His eyes followed the ad back into her cleavage.

"They probably don't want people who say *fuck* neither." She kicked the seat in front of her, then held up the mirror, smiling with her mouth closed. "How's this?"

It wasn't easy talking without your lips, like that wooden dummy at the county fair. "You into wood?" he'd asked her, lipless. An eyelid dropped in a slow wink. Even a guy made out of a tree couldn't resist her.

She sucked in her top teeth. She'd just have to say less and zip it up to smile. "I got till tomorrow mornin' to get these babies white." She threw the mirror into her purse. "I need a cigarette. You got one?"

"You have six hundred and ninety-nine dollars?" Mayo asked her.

"No! Duh." She frowned. "Think I'm stupid? I got a credit card."

His face lit up. "Come." He reached for her hand. "We go to Las Vegas. You bring me luck."

She elbowed him. "Buzz off, joker."

He put a hand over his heart. "You believe in fate?"

It was the first time she'd actually looked at him. He was a skinny little runt with pleading brown eyes and a spiky mustache dotting his upper lip. His teeth were grayer than hers, pointy as a picket fence. They made her hate him a little bit less.

"For real?" she answered him. "I do."

He clapped his hands. "I want to marry you."

She snorted. "Yeah. Get in line." She peered over Snuggles and yawned. "Where the hell are we anyway?"

She'd taken her last downer before leaving Umpire and it was starting to wear off. She had to have a cigarette and soon or she'd be jumping out of her skin. And besides, she was broke.

\* \* \*

The sun was low in the sky when the bus pulled into the Texarkana station. Even before the wheels had stopped, she was up and pushing past Mayo.

"Keep your mitts off Snuggles or I'll kick your ass."

"*Sí, mi amor.*" Mayo trotted off the bus behind her.

The smokers were already lighting up behind the station. A hefty black man in a blue toboggan cap wore strings of jeweled crosses around his neck. His bulging forearms were tattooed with thorns. She asked him for a smoke and he shook out his pack. They were menthol, but she took two anyway. He lit one of them with his Bic. Mayo hung close by, watching. His pants sagged low on his hips, the cuffs bunched on the ground. She turned her back on him and locked eyes with the muscleman.

"Man." She exhaled long. "Is this bus borin' or what?"

The muscleman chuckled down in his lungs. "You got that right, princess."

She glowed at him. "You got to make your own fun, know what I sayin'? That is one thing I am good at." Twenty bucks would get her a pack of cigarettes and something to eat.

The muscleman flashed a gold front tooth. "Me? I'm good at Jesus."

She'd heard that one before. "Didn't Jesus like to party?"

"Water into wine, baby." He put his fingers to his eyes. "Lord, lead me not," he whispered, loud enough for her to hear. He looked her in the face. "You need money, princess?"

This was going to be easier than she thought. "Ten bucks. I can pay you back. Seriously. I'm gonna be rich."

"Ain't we all?" He threw down his cigarette. "You can have my money. But have you got God? I want to pray with you. Will you let me do that?"

"You know what?" she answered. "Twenty would be better."

The muscleman took her hands in his. His eyes were closed. She still had the cigarette between her lips. She blew smoke out of the side of her mouth and lowered her beautiful head.

\* \* \*

There were more people in the Texarkana station than lived on her entire road in Umpire. With the twenty she weaseled off the muscleman, she bought a pack of cigarettes. The price was a total rip-off, so she slipped a Bic and some Chap Stick into her pocket to even things up a little.

Mayo trailed her. She ignored him. At the food counter she ordered a burger, French fries and a cherry coke. The lady who took her order had a red beehive all gelled up like her ex-stepmother's plastic couch.

Until her food came, there was nothing else to do but watch the weirdoes in the chairs. That brown old couple had to be foreigners. They had a cooler with plastic containers of strange-smelling food and icy bottles of water. The man wore a yellow suit, bright as a balloon. The woman had on this crazy red-blue-green flowing thing that hung off one shoulder. A gray braid fell to the back of her knees. There was a red dot on both their foreheads. The girl figured they had to be Catholic or something. Down the row from them slouched a bearded hippie in torn overalls and a Harley-Davidson t-shirt, reading the *Old Testament*. That guy definitely needed to get a life.

A fat man came in the station with a dog, a real dog, a black one, in a harness worn as a pair of thrift store slippers. The dog kind of reminded her of this old mutt her daddy had. Till he got drunk and ran over it twice. This dog here was so old and tired, he could hardly move. She wondered if the fat man had to buy a ticket for *his* dog. They were stopped in the middle of the room like they had nowhere to be. She went over to them, smiling with her mouth shut.

"Mister, can I pet your dog?" she asked, between closed lips.

The fat man threw back his head. "He's working."

She took that for a *yes*. The dog lowered his rump. She bent to rub his ears, giving them both a free view of her boobs. The fat man stared at the ceiling and the dog pretty much acted like she wasn't there either. She figured the guy was queer as a three-dollar bill and that mutts didn't know about beautiful.

The beehive lady waved at her from behind the counter. It was about time. She moved off from the fat man and his clueless dog.

"Stop." The lady cupped her hands around her red mouth. "Take his arm."

79

"What?"

"I. Said. Take. His. Arm."

"What for?"

"Can't you see? He's blind."

So *that* was his problem. She'd never seen a blind person before, not up this close and for real. The fat man swung his chin. His lids fell back. His eyeballs ricocheted in their sockets like metal balls in a human pinball machine.

The beehive lady waved again. "Bring him over here. He always gets something to eat with me."

The girl didn't know what to do next. She answered, "O. K.," loud and slow.

The fat man tilted his head back and forth like he was laughing. His eyes spun. "I'm blind, not deaf," he told her. "Give me your arm."

She stuck her arm straight out in front of him. The fat man zeroed in on it with a sweaty palm. The dog got to his feet and the three of them sidestepped to the counter in one stuck lump like pieces of taffy melted together in the sun.

The beehive lady cooed to the fat man. "What you having today, sugar? The usual?"

The fat man knew her voice and obviously loved it. He lifted his head, eyes rolling, mouth stretched. The usual turned out to be fries with chili and extra cheese and a raw cheeseburger with no bun for the dog.

The beehive lady winked at the girl. "I got him now, sugar. Here's your food. That'd be six forty-three."

The girl handed over a ten. The beehive lady bounced away to get her change. She cut her eyes at the fat man. His skin was white as skim milk and he had thin boring hair. He didn't even seem to know she was there anymore and for sure that dog didn't. She could give them both the finger and it wouldn't faze them one bit.

The fat man put a hand in his pants pocket and brought out a big wad of folded bills. His fingers felt along the edges. Each five had a corner turned over. He pulled out two of them and the rest went back in his pants. He sniffed the air. "You smell funny."

"Huh, what?" The girl glanced around. "Who you talkin' to? Your dog?"

"No. You. You smell like stale smoke."

Her mouth flew open but nothing came out. The beehive lady hustled back with her change and the dog's uncooked cheeseburger. The girl grabbed the money and the food. She plopped down in a chair beside the brown old couple. She wasn't hungry anymore. She glanced back at the counter. The fat man and the beehive lady were still flirting with each other. The dog lay at the man's feet, licking the floor where his cheeseburger had been.

She left her food on the chair. From out of nowhere Mayo pounced on it. "Wait!" he called after her, pointing at the food. "*No quierás?* You do not want?"

She didn't bother to answer but instead went out to smoke what she swore would be her last.

*     *     *

When the bus to Nashville was called, she stayed where she was on the platform. She twirled her new lighter and finished her smoke. Not until every other passenger was on the bus, did she toss the butt and run for it. Mayo swerved in behind her and took his seat like before.

She glared at him. "Go bother somebody else for a change."

Mayo slurped on her cherry coke. "I am happy here."

She blew out her cheeks. "Hey! Do I smell?"

"Mm. *Sí*. Like a *flora*."

She groaned. "Listen, jerk" she growled, between clenched lips. "I'm gonna tell that driver if you don't leave me the fuck alone."

He shined his eyes at her. "Do not worry. I will not say about the lighter."

Kicking his legs out of the way, she stomped down the aisle. "That creep is botherin' me," she told the new driver.

"Which creep would that be?"

The driver to Nashville was a short black woman with crimped orange hair and a small, cinched-in waist. She peered past the girl up the aisle. Marcos-or-Mayonnaise waved back at her.

"Who that?" The driver laughed. "That's Marcos Jimenez, doll. He's through here all the time. His wife lives in Nashville. He's harmless."

The girl folded her arms. "I don't want him by me."

The driver looked at her and smiled. "You ought not to frown like that, baby girl. Whyn't you come down here and sit by me? I got a seat all picked out for you."

The girl tore back to rescue Snuggles. She didn't give Mayo so much as a good-riddance glance. Rushing down the aisle with the poodle over her head, she followed the driver's lacquered fingernail to a seat across the aisle.

The fat man was sitting by the window. She stamped her foot; this wasn't what she had in mind. The bus was already backing out of its lane. The driver tapped the brakes. The girl lurched forward.

"Sit down," the driver ordered her. "Before you hurt your beautiful self."

The girl dropped into the seat beside the fat man. His knee went up against hers. There was hardly enough room for her, let alone Snuggles. He swiveled his head. "You again."

This was definitely the last time she was taking the bus. It'd be limos only, from here on out. "Where is your dog?" she asked, not that she cared.

The fat man pointed down. She bent to find the mutt lying under the seat behind their feet. He looked to be asleep or dead. "Shit," she scoffed. "He must be like a hundred years old."

"He's four."

"Nuh-uh. What's his problem?"

"He's working. You take the harness off him and he's all over the place."

"Huh." She didn't know what the hell he was talking about. "I got a dog too," she informed him.

"At home?"

"Nope. Here. You want to pet him?"

He nodded and waited. She pulled on his sleeve and brought his hand over to Snuggles. When his fingers touched the pink fur, she shook the dog and growled. The fat man jumped. He swung his hand away.

She snorted. "I'm sorry. I'm bad. He don't bite, I swear. He's fake."

"Fake?" His spider-like fingers came back to the dog. "Soft."

"Yeah. And pink."

"What is pink?"

"Pink. You know. Pink!" She stared at him. "Lips are pink. Your tongue is pink. Pigs are pink."

His chin went up. "Pig is delicious."

All of a sudden she felt like crying. She peered back at Mayo. He was asleep on the shoulder of a round black woman. Her head was covered in a flowery scarf and she was sleeping, too.

The girl buried her face in Snuggles' neck. They had seven more hours to go. It'd be the middle of the night before they got to Nashville. They didn't have a place to stay, if you didn't count the bus station. She'd have to wash up in the bathroom in the morning and put on her best outfit – a pants suit of fake white leather with the fringes and real rhinestones – to get to the Institute of Beauty and Po-easy in time.

Her hand slipped into her tank top to feel the ad between her tits. She repeated the words to herself. She couldn't understand why fate had put her next to a guy who didn't know what pink was. She glanced at him. He wasn't staring out the window or listening to music or doing anything, far as she could tell. His head went up and down with the bump-bump of the bus.

Keeping her lips together, she said, "Guess you don't know what po-easy is neither."

"Spell it."

She took out the page. The bus was as dark inside as it was out. "You know what, driver?" she called. "I can't see a fuckin' thing."

"Me neither." The fat man giggled.

The driver laughed with him. "There's a reading light above you, darlin'."

Of the two buttons on the ceiling over her head, one had a drawing of a light bulb. She pressed that one and a feeble light came on.

"P-O-I-S-E," she spelled out.

"Oh. Poise. It means – you know, cool. Confident."

"Oh. Yeah. I knew that."

She put the ad back in her bra. She wasn't feeling too cool about her teeth right now. She took the mirror from her purse. Her teeth were as gray as three-day-old cigarette ash.

"I don't suppose you got any tooth whitener on you?"

"Why? I need some?" The fat man snickered and then asked, "Where you going?"

"Nashville."

"Me too. You live there?"

"I do now." She flipped her hair. "I'm goin' to modelin' school."

"Oh. Why?"

She gasped. "Why? Because. Duh. I'm beautiful."

"I don't know what that is."

She had the awfulest feeling then, like in a dream when she stepped off a curb and there was nothing under her foot. Usually that woke her up but not this time. This time she was already awake and sinking, sinking through the seat, through the fat man's dog, though the bus and the pavement moving below it. There was nothing to break her fall and nobody there to be broken.

"Here." Seizing the fat man's hand, she brought his fingers to her face. "This is beautiful."

His hand hesitated. He slid slow fingers along her eyebrows and across her lashes. Trembling, his hand moved down her nose and downy cheeks. She held her breath. His touch was light as cat whiskers. No one had ever touched her like that before.

He stopped at her lips. "Pink," he whispered. "Beautiful."

She closed her mouth before he could see her teeth. And then it hit her. The fat man couldn't see how messed up her teeth were. He had no idea. To him, she wasn't just beautiful, she was perfect.

Her hand went around the back of his neck. She brought his head down to hers and kissed him on the mouth. His lips were thin and squishy. She slid her tongue between them.

The fat man pulled away, rubbing his lips. "That tickles."

She removed her hand from his neck. "I don't know why I did that."

He laughed, a funny choking sound. "Am I beautiful?"

"Let me see," she replied.

She ran her fingers down his face, down his crazy useless eyes and splotchy nose, down his pasty cheeks and odd little nub of a chin. Her hand slowed. She tapped his cheek.

"Yeah," she lied. "You are."

# One-Way to Blythe

———◆•◆•◆———

"What you need this time, cowboy?"

The ticket agent's rap was friendly enough, only he wasn't fooled for a minute. He'd been to her counter before. The tan polyester uniform was stretched over her inviting curves like a second skin and those slate-gray eyes were colder than a lizard's.

The cowboy's battered straw Stetson bent toward her as if he were bowing. He stooped to place a guitar case between his boots. Upright, he was tall and large-framed, the muscles in his arms slack. His thrift-store denim jacket had a dirty white fleece collar and was so small on him it could have been a woman's, or a child's. The torn green t-shirt barely covered the belly roll breaking at his waist. Duct tape repaired his jeans at the knee. He looked to be about fifty, give or take twenty years. The angular bones of his face were softened by enormous watery blue eyes and a scraggly beard that often held clues to his last meal.

"Bus to California," he barked. He dumped a handful of crumpled dollars and loose change on the counter.

The agent laid a fist on the shelf of her hip. "And what? Just drop your skinny butt at the border?"

He grunted, amused. "Los Angeles."

"Oo-wee." The agent swung her hands over the keyboard in front of her. "He takin' his bad self to Hollywood."

The cowboy watched her talons click across the keys. The tips were an inch long, diagonally striped red, white and blue. They made him want to salute.

"Round trip?" she inquired, already knowing the answer. The man was always going somewhere on a one-way ticket, only to return mysteriously to her counter to set out again.

"How much?" he replied, playing along.

She slung her weight from one hip to the other. "Austin to L.A.? Three hundred and eighty-two dollars."

"What?" He lifted his hat to scratch a bald spot on the back of his skull. A lank ponytail dangled beneath it. "Cain't even afford to be poor no more."

He replaced the hat. "What's it one way?"

The agent shaped each word with professional patience. "One hundred and ninety-eight dollars."

The cowboy shrugged. "Guess you won't be seein' me agin."

"Uh-huh," the agent answered.

He proceeded to unfold each balled-up bill, pressing them flat on the counter and stacking them by worth. His nails were long and gritty, slightly curled at the ends. He picked up the first pile and licked his thumb. The counting began at a clip, slowed as the bills dropped in value, and stalled out completely at one hundred and seventy-four. Undaunted, he reached into a boot to slap two more one-dollar bills on the counter. Next he attacked the coins, trapping the quarters first and dragging them two-by-two from the heap.

The ticket agent eyed the line of travelers behind him. "Take your time, baby. Ain't nobody here but you got a bus to catch."

Ignoring the sarcasm but not the advice, his long fingers eked out three more dollars in change. Finally, he nudged the last two pennies forward, to make a grand total of one hundred and eighty dollars and eighty-seven –

He pounded the counter. "God damn it!" His arm swung to his back pocket to retrieve a lottery ticket which he presented to the agent. "Take it, sweet thang. You hit the jackpot, you send me half."

The agent dead-eyed him. "Are you messin' with me?" Her voice had jumped an octave.

The cowboy threw out his most persuasive smile. "I'll write a song 'bout you."

"This man is messin' with me," the woman declared to the ceiling.

He slumped on the counter. "Come on, pretty lady. Gimme a break."

"Do I look like the Bank of America to you?" Her question was directed to his hat.

The cowboy watched her from under its brim. Her bronze curls made a laminated helmet around the heart-shaped face. The helmet didn't move a hair when she swung back to the computer to tap-dance her nails across the keyboard again.

"One hundred and seventy-nine dollars will get your sorry behind all the way to Blythe, California," she informed him.

He lifted his chin. "How much further to L.A.?"

"About nineteen dollars." She swept the leftover coins in his direction. "Smile, baby, it's your lucky day."

"Yeah," he scowled, pocketing the lottery ticket. "Let's git married."

* * *

He never liked to check the guitar, didn't matter how far he was going. He'd found it in a pawn shop in San Antonio, paid for it with the boots he had on. Those boots were the canvas for his personal depiction of the Sermon on the Mount, painted in bright magic-marker colors and entitled *Six Flags Over Jesus*. He had walked barefoot out of that shop with the old guitar in his hand.

The thing was a genuine antique, judging by the splintered holes in the body, which he had repaired with duct tape. He appreciated that somebody had taken the time to take a nail and scrape the brand name off the neck. To his way of thinking, the less he knew about something, the rarer it became.

The times he needed some quick cash, he'd sell the guitar to a friend or a fan, and then borrow it back almost immediately. He'd gotten good at keeping it just long enough for the buyer to forget all about it or get tired of asking for it, whichever came first. The cash for California was drummed up the same way, with the promise to return the guitar to its new owner by the end of this month.

It was the one thing he'd held onto in his life and he didn't care to be parted from it. Consequently, he'd learned to do lots of things one-handed. That came in useful on lonely nights, of which there were many. Or when driving a stick shift and rolling a joint. Or while carrying the guitar and lighting a smoke in line for the westbound bus.

Usually, the line for California formed inside the station in front of Gate 3. Waiting there always provided the opportunity to peruse the mural painted on the entire wall between the two washrooms at the back of the station. The artwork reminded him of his own, which he referred to as *Thou Art*. The panorama on the wall portrayed a bevy of religious rock stars: the sainted Mary and Joseph on camels, looking for some place to give birth, and sharing the Way with a pair of zoot-suited skeletons stepping out for *Día de Los Muertos*, the Day of the Dead.

This afternoon, however, with so many passengers waiting to board, the driver had already pulled the line out onto the loading platform. The cowboy grimaced; he was no fan of this particular driver. The man made him think of an albino pear – being wide at the waist, narrow at the shoulder and white from stem to core. Coppery hairs stuck up from his scalp as if he'd been picked too soon.

The line moved forward. The guitar case hung from the cowboy's left wrist as if it was handcuffed there. His right hand took up the slack, removing a cigarette from behind his ear, sticking it between his lips, finding the matches stashed in his torn breast pocket. His big calloused thumb flipped the cover open and stood a paper match on its end. The red sulphur head was struck with the same flat thumbnail he used to pick the bass line. He blew out the flame with the first noisy exhale.

In front of him stood a slender soldier with cropped, shining hair. The cowboy tapped the soldier's shoulder. "This the bus to California?"

The soldier turned to the cowboy. Her gaze was direct. The girl had brown eyes like toasted almonds and a bowed, cupie-doll mouth.

"Darlin'," the cowboy added, placing his hat over his heart.

The soldier blushed. She squinted at her ticket. Her black hair was buzzed short in the back revealing a velvety nape. The longish fringe on top glistened in the shade of the platform.

"I'm going to Marfa," she allowed.

"Close enough." The cowboy sucked in his cheeks, dragging on the cigarette, and held his breath. "I was born in Marfa," he rasped.

The soldier nodded and moved up the line. She handed the driver her ticket. The driver's eyes were on the cowboy. His fingers snapped peevishly over the soldier's shoulder.

"Hey! You!" he yelled at the cowboy. "Put that smoke out! You want to blow up the bus?"

"Fascist," the cowboy muttered, ambling out of the line and over to the curb. He had a rocking gait. "I'm a vet you know."

The soldier's head snapped toward him. "Which war? Sir," she added.

He waved away the question. "I don't remember." He pointed to his forehead. "Brain injury."

The driver rolled his eyes and wobbled his head like a dashboard ornament, as if to warn the soldier not to believe a word this clown said. He inspected her ticket. "You get the military discount?"

"Yes sir."

The driver tore off the top page. "Change in Fort Stockton for Marfa."

The soldier took her ticket and boarded the bus without a backwards glance at either man. The driver turned to the cowboy, still at the curb, still puffing away in vigorous protest.

The driver clapped his hands once. "Let's go if you're going, pal. You're not making me late."

The cowboy stamped out the cigarette on the flapping sole of his boot. Sliding the butt behind his ear, he sauntered over to the driver as if they both had all the time in the world.

The driver flipped his ticket open. "California this time." He sounded bored.

"Yep." The cowboy nodded sagely. "Goin' to see my friend. Might even marry me a movie star."

The driver snorted. "Good luck with that." Brandishing a hole-punch like a pistol, he spun it twice and shot two circles into the top page of the cowboy's ticket. "Stay on till Blythe."

"I'm blithe now," the cowboy replied, bending over to shove the ticket into his boot.

\* \* \*

The bus from Austin to LA was packed. The cowboy headed for the last seat but it was already taken up by a family of sleeping Mexicans.

The father, mother, and two older children were wrapped around each other in a tangle of brown arms and legs. A baby slept on a silky purple jacket set out on the floor.

One row down and across the aisle, the soldier already lay across two seats. Her legs were at right angles to the window, her head propped up on the plastic arm rest.

The cowboy hovered over her. "Would it be unpatriotic of me to ask you to sit up?"

Her eyes opened. In this light they were the color of buttered toast. Without a word she tipped up and bounced over to the window. The cowboy crashed into the seat on the aisle. He tucked the guitar case under him and turned to admire the tumble of fruit pickers in the last seat.

"Now that's the way to travel," he opined to anyone in earshot.

The only reply came from the bus: four honks announcing its departure. The cowboy laid back. He watched the bus slip through the knot of bridges and roadways that had to be unraveled before it could get out of town. There was nothing he liked better than a pane of dirty glass between him and the backwards-sliding landscape. Leaving was always the best part of going – that sensation of liftoff, of horizons broadening, of feeling his hold on his life in Austin slip away like money.

The bus zigzagged through a maze of streets leading south and west away from the city. The cowboy slid the guitar case forward and took out a blue plastic bottle of Maalox. Pushing the case back behind his boots where he could feel it at all times, he took a long, slow, gulping swallow. Then, smacking his lips, he offered the bottle to the soldier.

She held up a hand. Her nails were bitten to the nubs. "No thanks."

The cowboy winked. "It's Jack."

"Hello Jack," she returned dully. "Mona."

His guffaw ended with a burp. "Not me, Mona. Him." He tapped the bottle. "Jack? As in Daniels?"

"Ah." She nodded but did not smile. "My mother would kill me if I came home stinking."

"Lucky for me," the cowboy replied. "My mother's dead."

He found this hilariously funny; he had no idea if it was true. He did know he used to love his mother – he hadn't made that up – when he was a kid and they had sung together. She was pretty then and sweet, playful at times. He and her and his older sister were a gospel trio, traveling around in a beat-up old Pontiac, singing for Jesus at churches, revivals, shopping malls. Their voices were a celestial blend; everybody said so, like they were some brand of Sunday morning coffee. They even sang on the radio once, though where that was he could no longer recall. Any more than he could remember when and where he had lost his mother's love.

He had a bad habit of showing up unannounced. It was one of those lessons he had to keep learning over and over. Even now, his friend in California had no idea he was coming. The urge to be somewhere else would burst over him and spread down his body like that man-eating blob in the sci-fi movie he'd seen as a youngster. There was no predicting what might bring it on: the tap of a Billy stick, an ugly break-up, usually with a dancer, or something as small as a busted guitar string. Alcohol couldn't cure it. The only rememdy that worked was getting out on the road.

He hadn't visited his mother in years maybe and then one after-noon he just showed up at her kitchen door in Missouri. *Misery*, he called it, *my mother lives in Misery*. She'd finally divorced his father, he couldn't blame her for that. He'd heard she remarried, a piano player from her church, and that was who she sang with now.

She had become an old woman. He had stared at his mother through the screen door, like she was a stranger he was visiting in prison. A starched halo of white hair encircled her head. Her powdered cheeks were sagging, her lips twitched with churchy disapproval. He saw himself as she did: string-haired, bearded, a tramp in rags and duct tape, looking for a handout no doubt.

"Mother," he said. "It's Mike."

They had the same eyes. It had come to him two nights ago in an alcohol-induced melancholy that his mom had given him the music and he'd never thanked her for it. So he'd picked up in the middle of the night and hitch-hiked through three states to come and tell her thanks. He was hoping they might sing together.

"Will you be staying for supper?" Those were her first words to him.

They didn't sing that night, nor did he stay for supper. He got back on the road before sunset, hitching a ride to anywhere in the dark.

*   *   *

He had gotten too old to hitch-hike. The reason, he told himself, was that the only people who'd pick him up anymore were middle-aged men who either wanted to fight him or date him or both.

A hoarse blow on the microphone scattered his thoughts. "Let me have your attention, please," the driver said. His voice was as tight as a new kindergarten teacher in cotton-crotch pantyhose on the first day of school.

"My name is Dave," he began. "That's D-A-V-E. Dave. Not Bus Driver. Not Mr. Bus Driver. Not Fatso. Dave. I will be your operator to El Paso."

In the back seat the Mexican family awoke and began chattering among themselves. They chirred like parakeets, speaking a soft, animated Spanish.

"I don't have a lot of pet peeves." Dave's voice rose above theirs. "But the main one is people talking when I'm talking. And just because you don't speak English doesn't mean you're not talking. So everybody listen up once and this won't take long. There are a few things we need to go over and we will have no trouble I am sure."

The family quieted. In the silence the cowboy belched volcanically. The soldier slipped an ear bud into her ear and set her cap over her eyes. She folded her arms above her stomach. Her bones were thin as straws. The cowboy couldn't picture her slinging an assault rifle, doing a hundred push-ups, or fending off a drunken lieutenant. He pulled his t-shirt down over his belly. It would be so easy now to lean over and kiss her.

Dave prattled on. "There is no smoking on this bus. There is no smoking on this bus. There is no smoking on this bus. Is there anyone who did not get that?"

Nervous laughter skittered through the bus. "Hey!" Dave exploded into the mike. "Whoever's playing their music up loud? I can hear that and I'm pretty much deaf in both ears from two stints in the military. So for sure the person next to you can hear it. Keep your music down. You're the only one wants to hear it. No alcohol. No loud voices. No profanity, which is just a thirty-dollar word for cussing. Oh yeah. And one more thing."

He punched every word. "All. You. Cow. Pokes. You got to use the john? Sit down on the seat. I don't care how many westerns you've seen, nobody ever shot nothing off the back of a moving horse. Any questions?"

"Yeah," the cowboy hollered up the aisle. "Can we smoke?"

A wave of titters rode his question to the front. Dave kept his voice even. "If you like walking."

"I been walkin.'"

The cowboy held up his boot to show the holes in his sole. He wore his poverty like a badge of honor and only occasional bitterness.

"Right," Dave pronounced. "So just shut up, chill out, and let me get us where we're going on time."

"Amen!" the cowboy cried, flinging a hand into the air and then collapsing into his seat, as though that last burst of enthusiasm had all but emptied him of air.

\* \* \*

He was going to have trouble sleeping. Which was a shame because riding the dog provided one of his more comfortable bunks. The seats were a hell of a lot softer than a blanket under a bridge and a whole hell of a lot drier than the dumpster behind the Vietnamese restaurant off The Drag.

The night before had been spent on the floor of a friend's back porch, trying to sleep off the night before that. That evening had been spent shooting speedballs in a shed in some stranger's backyard. He picked at the boils on his arm; his body was still leaching speed. His socks were wet, his feet itched him horribly. He'd begun to think of death as the absence of scratching.

On impulse he pulled off his boots. The ticket went under his hat. The socks came off with a yank, they were little more than rags. He tucked them into the strap across the seatback to dry. They gave off a smell that would make a buzzard gag.

The soldier bolted up. "Don't do that!" she exclaimed, waving her cap at the stench. "That crap is contagious. They court-martial you for shit like that."

"Oh, operator!" the cowboy called out in a prissy voice. "She's cursing!"

"Come on!" The soldier popped up in her seat to check out the driver. "I just got back," she whispered to the cowboy. "Give me a break. I book out in a month."

The cowboy held up the blue bottle. "I'll drink to that, Mona."

He took a slug and handed her the container. This time she took it, holding it with two fingers at arm's length as if it contained a urine specimen, or worse.

The cowboy got up barefoot, the socks hanging from his hand like hooked fish. He rocked to the bathroom, pushed open the door, and tossed the offending rags into the toilet. They made a small defenseless splash. Listing back to his seat, he pulled the boots on over his naked feet.

The soldier watched as he lifted his hat and put the ticket back in his boot. "You're not really a vet," she remarked.

"Veterinarian," he replied. "Circus animals."

"Get out." Her laugh was a girlish tinkle.

He took the Maalox bottle from her. "Seriously. I was drafted for Nam but it didn't take."

"Why's that?"

"Maybe 'cause I went down to the recruitment office with a hundred pipe cleaners taped to my body?"

She frowned. "Are you a pacifist or just crazy?"

"Both." He took another swig, then wiped his mouth with the back of his hand. "How many did you kill?"

The soldier's eyes slid to the window. "I'm a mechanic," she murmured, as if that were classified information.

The cowboy clapped a hand to his beard. "That's funny. I always think of mechanics as fat guys with no butt."

Her laughter chimed again. "I got the no-butt part down. Tanks, gun trucks, Humvees, you name it? I can fix it."

"And now you goin' to fix your mama's car."

"My mama don't have a car."

The soldier stretched out her legs and reset her cap over her eyes. Her birdy wrists were crossed over her waist like a closed sign. The cowboy took another gulp of whiskey. His head was starting to smooth out, his thoughts leveling to a distant hum, like a beehive one county over. He sat up straighter. He felt responsible for the soldier now, as if she was a child playing a dangerous game of dress-up.

* * *

The highway was taking them south and west across Texas. The lean hot rays of the lowering sun cast the shadow of the bus along the shoulder of the road. The black rolling rectangle swallowed up the grassy asphalt, the smashed armadillo shells, the black jagged rims of blown-out tires the truckers called *alligators*. The shadow on the shoulder rose and fell, fattening and thinning out the way his body had stretched and shrunk in the fun-house mirror of a traveling carny he'd visited as a kid in Odessa.

The bus shook like a horse-drawn buggy. The rattle in the rack above him sounded as if it was coming from somewhere inside his brain. His knees had nowhere to go. The left one swung in the aisle like an unlatched gate, while the other jutted into the space filled by the soldier's legs. He was careful not to touch her.

His hat slipped down over his eyes. In the dark waters behind his lids an alligator swam up, chased by an eighteen-wheeler driven by his dad. His father's muscled arm draped out the window, a lit cigarette stuck up from his fist. A strutting little bantam of a guy, daddy would be absent weeks, months, come home without warning, strung-out on pills, ugly and threatening to kill them all. They'd wait until he passed out on the floor and then they tiptoed into the Pontiac without closing the doors and set off down the road. Leaving had felt good then, too.

His sister had written him when their daddy finally bought it. That was fifteen years ago, the last time he'd had a word of her. In her letter she said their father had left this world lonely as a scarecrow in January – those were her exact words. The letter didn't reach him until weeks after the funeral. Not that it mattered. He wouldn't have gone anyhow; he had no respects to pay.

From the inside band of his hat he removed a creased and yellowing page, opening it with careful fingers. It had been folded and unfolded so many times the seams made a see-through lattice held together only by the loops and laces of his sister's handwriting.

"I wasn't really born in Marfa," he told the sleeping soldier.

They had just liked the sound of it, him and his big sister. Said fast, the word barked like a fox; spoken slow, it summed up lonesome. They had lived there for a time with their mother, before their daddy found them again, when his sister was already a teenager and he was still a squirt. The three of them would get up in the night and ride into those stark Davis Mountains. His mother sat alone in the backseat. She let him drive up there in those hills, even though he was too young for a driver's license. He had to sit on three Bibles to see over the dash. The windshield wipers on the old Pontiac had never worked right, so they rigged them with a wire hanger his sister operated out of the front window on the passenger side. She fiddled back and forth as he drove, the wipers clicking and clacking through the fog. In the cold damp dawn the car glided past tall rock towers that looked in the mist like children's castles made from wet sand. Wind-tossed tumbleweed scraped the road clean as a conscience.

His mother always said those Davis Mountains felt like the end of the world.

\* \* \*

The lights in the bus had been down a while. Outside, the road wound through dark hills mounded like sleeping bears furred with red chaparral. The new moon was so slim it might have been an accident, a slit in the sky letting in the radiance that lives behind the night.

The baby in the backseat had been crying a long time. One by one her family had cooed to her in gentle Spanish phrases. They offered her cheesy puffs to gnaw on that were a bright radioactive orange. Her cries were shrill. The tiny tongue throbbed in the empty mouth like a starving baby bird.

Passengers rustled in their seats. Only the soldier slept soundly, immune to any noise slighter than a bomb exploding. She was turned toward the window, her cap askew. The cowboy clutched the Maalox bottle; it was almost as empty as his mind. His thoughts rushed out in fits and starts, wandering from past to future to present and the miserable child behind him.

The overhead lights flickered on. "You need to shut that kid down." Dave's voice clipped over the baby's cries. "Or I'm going to have to put the whole lot of you out on the road."

The lights went out again. The cowboy twisted his body to peer at the family behind him. The woman holding the infant could have been its mother or its grandmother, her cheeks were lined as a city roadmap. She held the infant against her shoulder to muffle its sobs. Her black eyes glittered at the cowboy.

"*No más leche*," she murmured. She touched her breast with a clawed hand.

After a moment, the cowboy slid out the guitar case and turned his body into the aisle. The instrument rested against his thighs, the neck rising like a goose in flight. He adjusted the keys, plucked at the strings, tuning. Drunk, sober, it made no difference; his fingers always knew what to do.

His left hand fluttered over the frets while the right drew out a prancing melody, effortless as breath. His thumb moved up and down, up and down, between the stair-steps of notes and strings. Music was another kind of leaving. The thunk-thunk of his thumb was a needle stitching all the bewildering loss and regret into one harmonic fabric. Playing made him forget himself, if only for the length of the song, and the guitar was his perfect partner in this, the instrument of the only salvation the world had ever offered him.

The woman seated the baby on her lap to watch the cowboy play. The child's face was a small mocha pumpkin topped with silky black spikes. It put a finger up its nose and stared at the man's mesmerizing thumb. Its sobs melted to hiccups. After a while the infant slumped against the woman's breast and fell asleep. A tiny filmy bubble blew in and out of the unfilled nostril.

The cowboy's last notes drifted up from the guitar. In the hush that followed, he leaned forward to put the instrument away. At that moment the bus jerked off the road, the cowboy's head rammed against the seatback, and Dave announced a ten-minute smoke break.

The smokers got up, dazed by the sudden stop but happy for any chance to indulge. A few smiled back at the cowboy. He got up, too. The soldier was still curled against the window. He turned to the woman behind him.

"Watch my guitar? *Por favor.*"

Four smiling heads nodded back at him as if they were all growing on the same neck. The cowboy took the cigarette butt from behind his ear. He mashed it between his lips and swayed down the aisle like a blind man, grabbing handfuls of seatbacks.

Dave stood beside the steering wheel, waiting for him. His face was a bright, angry pink. "Don't play that thing on my bus again," he growled.

The cowboy lifted his hat and dropped it back on his head. "You're welcome, Fatso."

\* \* \*

The new moon had set long before, deepening the night at the edge of the road. Like dice, the stars were flung loosely across the black sky. They cast a faint cold light over far-off ridges notched and pointed as arrowheads.

The cowboy sat on a picnic-table bench, hands in his pockets. He had smoked his last butt down to filter and ash. Dave stood near the bus, smoking, his eyes on the cowboy. He watched the cowboy suck the final drop from the blue bottle and toss it into a trash barrel. The plastic popped against a crumpled can. The cowboy reached over and shook the can. Beer sloshed in the bottom, so he downed that, too. Then he threw the can on the heap with a defiant flourish and burped his way back to the bus. Dave threw away his smoke and trailed the cowboy up the steps, close enough to rake his heels.

The cowboy wheeled around. "You need to learn you some manners."

Dave smirked. "Think so, do you?" He examined the cowboy's face as if he was memorizing it off a wanted poster.

"I know so."

The cowboy lurched up the aisle. His seat rolled under him as the bus jimmied out onto the highway again.

The soldier was awake now. She parted slivers of ebony hair with her fingers. Blinking, she warbled, "I like that song."

"I wrote it." There was no swagger in his reply.

She snorted like a pony on a cold morning. "You did not."

"Bet you five dollars." He held out a hand.

She stared at his palm. "Why aren't you famous?"

"Maybe I am."

"Let me see your driver's license."

He put a coy finger to his mouth. "I need to get around to that sometime."

"You could be rich," she insisted.

He shook his head. "I drink too much."

"That is so sad."

The cowboy's features sharpened like a falcon trained to prey on human pity. "I tell you what's sad," he scowled. "Sad is wars people make money on and them ones that help 'em do it. So don't think you don't kill 'cause you do."

The soldier's eyes darkened like buds about to bloom. "And you don't?" she whispered, rolling away toward the window.

A dry, sour taste filled the cowboy's mouth. The rattle above his head entered his brain like a drill, releasing the padlock on his memory with a click. Somewhere a door sang on a broken hinge, heavy footsteps clumped down a hall, there was the stink of diesel. His father's shadow slipped past his bedroom door and into his sister's room. Black branches leafed out on the wall. Behind his head someone was pleading. He could not move. Someone was sobbing. He prayed to Jesus who did not come. The cries pierced his skin like nails – and then everything stopped but the crying.

The bus had pulled off the road again. Over the baby's sobs the cowboy heard Dave pronounce, "I cannot have that child keeping my passengers awake. You people will have to get off here."

The cowboy catapulted out of his seat as if it was spring-loaded. He slammed down the aisle, shrieks of alarm following him like small exploding flares. He threw himself, snarling, at Dave.

"I'd rip out your heart if you had one."

Dave's hand went down beside his seat. The door opened with a feral hiss. "Get off my bus." The driver's voice was deadly cold.

The cowboy drew himself up. "I wouldn't stay on this fuckin' bus if it was the last ride to the Pearly Gates –"

Dave stood, facing him. The cowboy seesawed back. "I'll just git my guitar and be outa here –"

Dave's arm lowered like a mechanized roadblock. "We'll leave it for you at the next station."

"The hell you will."

The cowboy took a slow swing at Dave. His hand boomeranged, looping through the air and back toward his own chin. The driver's arm made a noose around the cowboy's neck. He dragged him to the floor. The cowboy flailed, the Stetson rolled off his head. He bumped down the steps and Dave kicked him out the door.

The cowboy sprawled face first in the dirt and got up sputtering. "Gimme the guitar! Give me it! It don't belong to you!"

As if in answer, his hat sailed out the door and landed at his feet. Dave's voice followed it. "The guitar will be waiting for you at Fort Stockton."

"Thief!" The cowboy lunged at the closing door. The bus began to pull away. He banged on its side. "Thief! Thief!"

Bus windows went by, each framing a different face, each face wearing the same shocked expression. In the last frame the soldier's wet cheek was mashed against the pane. She held up the guitar case for the cowboy to see.

"Marfa," she mouthed, pointing to the guitar, and then to herself. "I'll take it to Marfa." Her breath clouded the glass and then the bus was gone.

The cowboy chased the bus until it disappeared over a crest in the highway. He stopped, panting, kicking at a flume of exhaust. His boot flew off into a ditch. His ticket flapped away like a white bird in dark woods. He pulled off the other boot and tossed it in the opposite direction.

He leaned over his knees. His heart was knocking against the trap of his ribs. The double line under his bare feet narrowed to the horizon like an arrow pointing to nowhere. Without the guitar, his hand felt severed. The cowboy crumpled, holding his wrist. The night was vibrating – stars, leaves, rocks, dirt – everything was moving and alive. In the distance an oval tray of silver clouds grazed the tops of tall rock towers dimly lit from behind, as if the moon were parked on the other side of them. He had come again to the end of the world.

Leaving was never the problem. It was the staying put, the not-doing anything – that's what could kill you. He lay down on the asphalt, still warm from yesterday's sun, and waited for death or morning, whichever came first.

# Truth or Consequences

<hr />

*Mi gallo se murió ayer*
*Mi gallo se murió ayer*
*Ya no cantará coco rí coco rá*
*Ya no cantará coco rí coco rá*
*Mi gallo se murió ayer*

The song would not stop looping in Milos' head. Over and over it had played since Albuquerque, while his eyes stayed fixed on the red desert, gazing at nothing. To the east the Rio Grande ribboned south to Mexico under a turquoise sky and below the generous expanse of blue, the sandy scrublands were etched with ripples, like the ebbing of an ancient seabed. Milos did not notice any of these things. His attention was given to the singsong lullaby circling and circling. That alone could make him forget the unholy thing he had done.

*Mi gallo se murió ayer.* My rooster died yesterday. It was his father's voice singing the sad tale to him. *Ya no cantará coco rí coco rá.* Now he no longer sings cock-a-doodle do, cock-a-doodle do. That voice and the childish verse had pursued Milos onto the bus. He had four more hours till El Paso. His father was following him home.

Milos' handsome face bore the stamp of Spanish *Conquistadores.* He wore a purple-and-white-plaid cowboy shirt and a ten-gallon hat the color of maize. His braid pressed along his spine. Bending forward, he swung the knotty rope of hair free. It curled down his broad chest and across his thighs like a sleeping snake. Stones and metal disks were twined here and there in the shiny black coil. In Milos' twenty-eight years it had only been cut once.

*Mi gallo se murió ayer.* Memories were woven into the melody like the ornaments in his hair: *Papi's* leathery face bending over him, singing to him in his crib. Milos could not say if he really remembered this, or if he had been told the story so many times, it had hardened into memory. A memory as true as his father's sly imitation of a rooster, ruffling up his feathers, crowing at the dawn.

*Ya no cantará coco rí coco rá.* When he was older and could talk, Milos would shout out, "Cock-a-doodle-do!" while his father sang, "*Coco rí coco rá*" – as if to remind his *papi* that he, Milos, belonged to two worlds. That much he knew was real. And real, too, was the rough tickle of his father's braid, a braid as old as Milos himself. His father had begun growing his hair the day his first son was born, the same day Milos began growing his.

"It's not a Latino thing." Milos had heard him say this a thousand times over. "More like father-son."

*Mi gallo se murió ayer.* Death could not still his father's voice. Milos heard *Papi* trotting him off to kindergarten at age five, Milos with a braid to his shoulders, a note from the family priest, and terror in his heart. Father Juan had written the principal to say that Milos' braid was sacred to the Cordero family and if God did not object, surely the school would not either. The principal sent Milos home early. He could not guarantee the boy's safety if the other students bullied him. *Papi* flew into a rage. He threatened the principal personally with a lawsuit. When the school district superintendent advised the principal to back down, every boy in Milos' kindergarten class began growing a braid.

*Ya no cantará coco rí coco rá. Papi* never sidestepped a fight. Nothing prevented him from doing what he felt was right. When he died, his braid hung below his knees. In twenty-eight years it had not been cut once.

Milos did not cry when he saw his father lying in his casket yesterday. He did not cry now at the thought of him. Dead at sixty of complications from Agent Orange, his father wore his Vietnam army medals on his lapel, as requested in his will. His braid was tucked under him, out of sight. And Milos had not asked his mother, or his sisters, if that was the funeral home's decision, or his father's.

*   *   *

The blue-haired woman got on in the small *turista* town of Belén, which is Spanish for Bethlehem. Her long leather skirt wisped up the aisle with every step. Under her arm she carried a small wooden drum decorated with antlers. The woman had a face like a totem carved in polished sandstone, sharp-eyed, straight-nosed, full-lipped. The sides of her head were freshly shaved, the topknot swept up into a black crest with cobalt blue tips. Hawk-feathered earrings dipped in silver hung from her earlobes.

She looked like a rooster. An exotic female rooster, if such a thing could exist. Milos jammed his hand against his mouth and pretended to cough. He did not want to offend her by laughing out loud.

The woman ignored him. Settling in a seat one row down and across the aisle, she deposited the drum in the window seat. As Milos watched, she lifted her fringed arms and brought the lacy blouse up over her head. Milos glimpsed sinewy shoulders, forearms, wrists. Her bare breasts were small and hard with darkly-pegged nipples. Throwing on a pale sweatshirt, the woman squeezed her breasts through the fabric, then swiveled abruptly to stare at Milos.

The suddenness of her ferocity pinned his eyes to hers. He held her look for as long as he could but she was the stronger. His gaze retreated to the window, only to be drawn back in time to see her turn away in dismissal. Now he was free to inspect her profile: the generous mouth, the velvety scalp, the black-and-blue coxcomb. She swiveled her neck and folded into the seat, her spine curving away from Milos like a seashell.

She was maybe the most beautiful woman he had ever seen. He shut his eyes. His father's voice had been completely driven from his mind. The stranger disturbed him in a way few women did. It was not only her bizarre resemblance to a *gallo,* or the ease with which she took off her clothes. She had a fearless directness that made him want to resist and surrender all at the same time.

"Hair is powerful magic."

The voice was the purr of a puma. Milos' eyes jolted open. The rooster-woman had taken the seat beside him so quietly she could have been made of air. Instinctively his hand closed around his coil of hair. Beneath the blue coxcomb, the woman's eyes roved the length of Milos' braid. Her eyes were black and shiny as obsidian, with a thin rim of icy blue around the irises.

"Then why shave it off?" Milos was surprised by his bluntness.

"Less is more, *amigo.*" She extended ringed fingers. "Candy?"

"What?" Milos was caught off-guard. "No. Thank you."

She crowed. "My name. Is Candace Roughfeather. Candy to some."

She had a bewitching smile. Her teeth were edged in gold. The hand she gave to Milos was thick as a man's and bony, with blue corded veins. Her handshake was strong and mercifully brief.

Milos found his tongue. "Where are you going?" He was already envisioning them getting off together in El Paso.

"Truth or Consequences."

"Ah." So this was who went to the spa town that had named itself after a TV game show. "What do you do there?"

"Lie."

Milos chuckled. Candy smiled up at the ceiling. "Hey," she crooned. "Got any secrets you only tell strangers on a bus?"

The blood rose to Milos' face. She was gazing at him like she already knew what they were. He said the first thing that came into his head.

"Yeah, my grandfather was a bigamist."

Candy cackled like a hen. "I got one of them. We all got one of them, *amigo*. That's not a secret, that's a fact of life."

A stab of annoyance creased Milos' brow. "Then what's your secret?"

"I like to iron," Candy answered lightly and went back to her seat.

Milos felt duped. Candy Roughfeather – what kind of name was that, *amiga*? The woman was obviously *loco*. What did she know about his grandfather? Or the fact that his *Abuelo* had moved his mistress and her children into the second floor of the house where he lived with his wife and daughters on the first? It was a secret everyone knew. Like the illegal cockfights in his basement.

Images tumbled through Milos' mind. He saw his family dressed up, going with *Papi* to *Abuelo's* house on a respectably shabby street outside Albuquerque. The basement was always crowded with well-heeled spectators. And there was *Abuelo*, dignified in a white silk suit, reminding his gamblers in crisp, authoritative Spanish that women and children were also present, so no drinking, no fighting, no swearing.

Milos allowed himself a smile. *Abuelo's* speech was much like the driver's on leaving Albuquerque this morning. Only unlike *Abuelo*, the driver did not mention the *enchiladas* and *limonada* ready for purchase from his wife and daughters upstairs on the first floor. Refreshments that had been prepared by the family living on the second floor.

Two stories down, in the basement *plaza de gallos,* the cocks rose and fell, shuffling through the air, slicing and stabbing each other with bayoneted spurs. The duels were surprisingly clean. The roosters' gauzy feathers staunched the flow of blood, so none would spray the pale Sunday dresses of the beautiful *señoras.*

A cascade of white feathers transported Milos to the shed in the scrublands where he had helped his father train *Abuelo's gallos.* To make the roosters mean, the trainers kept them from their hens. Naturally the *gallos* blamed the next cock they saw for their deprivation. Preferably this happened in the pit. Cockfighting, *Abuelo* liked to say, was all about sex.

Milos clutched a white rooster in his hands as his father showed him how to run the hen-starved bird across a table for exercise, how to throw it in the air and let it flap down to work its wings and strengthen them. Milos' fingers held the rooster's crimson coxcomb and wattles while *Papi* sliced them off with a razor. And he heard him say to the *gallo* as he did every time, "For your own good. Otherwise there is too much for the other cock to grab in the pit."

At twelve Milos had performed a similar operation on his braid. That morning he had woken to snow in the yard, a short-lived miracle. The sprinkling of flakes turned out to be feathers, white ones everywhere. His father's prize gamecock was found half-chewed, lifeless as a *piñata* spilling guts instead of sweets, a demeaning death for so courageous a hero.

*Papi* was furious. He accused Milos' dog *Ocho* – so named for his eight distinctive spots – of murdering his champion. That was the last time in his life Milos could remember crying. His father drove the three of them out into the desert, Milos in the front seat holding *Ocho* and sobbing, begging *Papi* not to do what he knew he was going to do. The car swerved off the road. Slamming on the brakes, *Papi* ordered Milos to let the dog out. Milos refused. His father opened the door and pushed the dog into the dirt. The first shot flipped *Ocho* up in the air. He fell in a heap and did not move again.

At home Milos took a steak knife and cut off his braid at the neck. "In this country," he shouted at his father, "you are innocent until proven guilty!" The dog had been around *gallos* all his life, had never done such a thing before.

"Hypocrite!" Milos flung the braid at *Papi's* feet. "I loved that dog. You did not love that rooster." He had seen his father reach into the pit during a fight and snap the neck of a celebrated *gallo* the first time it backed away from a challenger.

*Papi* was devastated. For him the dog's execution was a simple matter of economic honor. The *gallo* had put food in his family's mouths, including the dog. Now the rooster was dead, so the dog had to pay with his life.

The next day a neighbor came over to confess that in fact it was *his* dog that had killed the bird. Milos and his father had still not forgiven each other for their mutual hotheadedness, when here came Ocho limping down the road, a clean bullet hole in his haunch. It was a miracle of mercy, a father-son thing.

Milos began growing back his braid. But the old bond between father and son had been frayed by their bloodless betrayals. Milos stopped attending the cockfights. *Papi* scoffed at his son's shyness with girls. It would take a lifetime to mend the new mistrust between them. And not even a lifetime had been enough. Shame washed over Milos, recalling his brazenness at his father's funeral yesterday.

He glanced at the rooster-woman's sinuous silhouette. Milos did not believe in signs but her appearance at this moment, and the confused feelings she stirred in him, had caught him unaware. Maybe he was *loco,* too. She had seen through his torment. What would she do if he told her his secret?

\* \* \*

"I stole my father's braid from his dead body."

Milos had crossed the aisle in one stride and was whispering in Candy's ear. Her eyes glinted open. "Do you have it with you?"

Milos nodded. Candy slipped into the window seat. The drum went on her lap. "Sit," she commanded.

He sat. The woman fanned her hands on the drum skin and waited. Milos stammered through his story. The idea had come on him like a flash flood through an *arroyo*. Was it foolish of him to expect to see his father's braid across his body in his coffin? Its absence was like a blade to his heart. All these years he had grown his hair believing he and *Papi* would get a second miracle. The funeral was his father's last chance to make one. Instead he had chosen to ignore his son, as if Milos had never existed.

Shaken, Milos had asked for time alone with *Papi*. When the room cleared, he approached the coffin. He would never know where he got the *cojones* to lift his dead father's head and saw off his braid with his pocketknife.

"For your own good," he told him. "So there will be less for the devil to grab in the pit." *Papi's* braid belonged to him now. He would be guilty until proven innocent.

Milos grew silent. Candy held out a bejeweled hand. "Give me the knife."

Milos hesitated. He shook his head to clear it. He had just bared his soul to this woman, and now he was afraid to arm her?

She gestured impatiently. Milos felt his will loosen. He handed her the knife. Candy placed a finger under an eye and pulled the lower lid down in a gesture of caution. "They throw your ass in jail for carrying shit like this on the bus you know."

She mumbled a few words over the knife and tucked it in her belt. "We'll need it for later," she explained. "Now. Get me your father's hair."

Milos wanted to protest. He opened his backpack on the rack above his seat and removed the red bandana he had wrapped around *Papi's* hair after the funeral.

Candy unfolded the cloth. Chemotherapy had withered his father's braid to a pile of thorny strings. She pressed the hair to her breast and began to chant in a low-throated language unknown to Milos.

A sharp pain ripped through his chest. "Stop!" he shouted.

Candy put a finger to his lips. "Shh. The ancestors are speaking through me." Her eyes darted over her shoulder. "Some say it's a gift. Others call it schizophrenia."

Milos' head spun toward her. Maybe he should not have given her the knife.

Candy's eyes narrowed. She pushed his head back with the heel of her hand. "Close your eyes. Listen. What do you hear?"

Milos' chest expanded. He feared it might implode. His father's voice burst into his mind. He began to sing: *Mi gallo se murió ayer. Mi gallo se murió ayer. Ya no cantará coco rí coco rá. Ya no cantará –"* Tears spilled down his cheeks. He could not sing another word.

Candy pressed her face to the glass. "Truth or Consequences. This is our stop."

Milos felt the bus slow under his knees. He swiped at his cheeks. "I'm going to El Paso."

Candy impaled him with her eyes. "Your father will never let go of you until you let go of him." She took hold of his braid. "We will burn them together."

The bus came to a stop. Candy dropped Milos' braid, stood him up and guided him down the aisle, through the bus door, and out into the hot bright desert air.

The dry breeze, and the growl of the departing bus, restored Milos' senses. He whirled in the parking lot. "What am I doing here?" he implored the sky.

"You don't trust me." Candy stood on tiptoe and kissed him full on the mouth. Milos felt himself surrender. He would do whatever she asked of him.

His fingers took her gently by the wrist. "You owe me a secret."

"It is only a secret to you," she purred.

Milos enfolded her in his arms. His hands slid around the taut ribs, the sculpted muscles of her waist. Candy leaned back in his embrace. Her hand brushed his cheek.

"You poor baby," she murmured. "*Coco rí coco rá.* I'm a man."

# A New York Minute

---•◦•---

Muwanda knew the old man was dying the second she put eyes on him. Tired as she was, she'd seen too much of death lately to start fooling herself about it now. Nothing was like before, in her other life, her *before* life, she called it. Before the storm.

The dying man came on in Mobile. Muwanda was laid out sound asleep across the last seat when he tapped on her shoulder and looked down in her face. Before the storm, she and her sisters had hired out with an agency in New Orleans called Blessed Hands, caring for white folks with more money and hurt than they knew what to do with. She had no idea where any of her patients were now. Like this old man here, she did not wish them ill. She just didn't have any more room inside her for any more pain. But her blessed eye had noted the man's ashy skin, thin as wax paper, and the blue-black lips like he'd been drinking ink. And his hair. The man had some strange hair. It was shiny yellow like a wet lemon. Hair dye, was her first thought; nobody want to get old. He lucky to be old, she told herself, rocking up and moving over to let him sit down.

The buses had started running again two days ago. This one was full down to the last two seats in the back. Muwanda took to the aisle where she could stretch her legs wide and the old man tottered past her knees to sit by the window. He had that smell, that nauseating blend of feces, neglect and decay that coats the walls of nursing homes where old poor folks go to rot. Muwanda fell back asleep, her generous body overflowing into the empty space between them.

She did not wake again till they were joined in Montgomery by a tall white lady and her cat. The cat was in a hot-pink pet carrier that went with the lady's otherwise sensible shoes. They had the same wide unblinking eyes, and the same hairdo – long straight silvery strands that flared up at the ends. And they simply had to sit by the window. Gumdrop was her service animal, the lady explained, though she didn't mention what service the cat actually provided. And Gumdrop needed something outdoorsy to look at or she would meow the entire way to Opelika. Nobody wanted that, so the old man slid in the middle between the two women and Muwanda's two-hundred-mile nap was officially over.

She had not slept so long or so hard since the day the Gulf entered her bedroom and carried her children's mattress out the back door. There'd be no more sleep now, not with that funky cross-eyed cat staring at her like a *Mardi Gras* voodoo mask, and this stinky old man with a foot out the door wrapped around her hip like one of her own.

Muwanda missed her kids. And she was comforted only by the vow she'd made to herself this morning: that she would be holding them again before this day was done.

\* \* \*

Right now, the old man was thinking, right now this minute, he could die and go happy. The bus could crash, it wouldn't matter. His contentment sprang, not only from his decision, long overdue, to go see his mother – there was also the jackpot of his current seating arrangement. Smitty didn't know how he'd come to be wedged between this fleshy woman of about forty he'd wager – a handsome black lady, head bound in a gold scarf, a black sweatshirt with the words NOLA RISING along her pillowy bosom – and this other new gal of maybe sixty-five who used to be a looker he could tell. And her cat. He didn't care one way or other about the cat. He could be dreaming the whole damn thing for all he knew. At ninety or ninety-one (if there was a birth certificate, Sammy Smith had never seen it), any woman who could still breathe looked like heaven to him and now here he was, hip-to-hip with not one but two.

Overcome with giddiness, Smitty smiled at his feet. He needed new slippers; these ones were worn through at the toe. He wiggled a big toe at himself and made a sound like walnuts cracking on the back of his tongue.

\* \* \*

"Let us all thank God we are in one piece and alive, hallelujah." This was how the bus driver greeted her new passengers boarding in Montgomery: eight storm refugees with no belongings and that nut-job with the cat. The cat lady had been a weekly on this schedule long before the storm.

The driver was a no-nonsense black woman down to, but not including, her nails which were a glittery blue-green like discreet bursts of fireworks at her fingertips. Ordinarily she'd never talk to her passengers this way but these were Biblical times. Turning out of the station, her fingers sparkled in the noonday light as she waved at the work crews with cherry-pickers and chainsaws, cutting up trees along the highway picked apart by the storm.

"That's right," Muwanda called from the back, shaking her gold-swathed head. She fanned a plump hand. "Sure enough." Her mild and easy delta drawl relieved each word of its harder consonants and curled every syllable at each end as if to soften the harsh existence that had given them life.

Everyone on the bus knew what the women were talking about. It had scarcely been a week since Hurricane Katrina gave Alabama a pummeling. And while the world stayed riveted on that business in New Orleans, anybody in the Hurricane Zone – basically the whole South – knew firsthand how murderous the storm had been. For at the same time Katrina was bringing New Orleans to its knees, five hundred miles to the north her outermost fringes were twisting into a deadly petticoat of lightning storms and tornadoes.

In Opelika, Alabama, Gumdrop's hometown, twenty houses, mostly trailers, had been destroyed and four people were killed. Across town from these tragedies, the prize irises in her owner's yard had been flattened by the downpour and would not be flowering this Thanksgiving. The storm had only directly affected them when Victoryland, the greyhound racetrack above Montgomery, was closed for a week to clean up the stadium so the dogs could race again. For years it had been their secret pleasure to sneak off to the track on the bus without anyone who mattered catching them at it.

Gumdrop's owner called herself Saudi. "Like half the country," she was quick to say; she thought that sounded witty. The nickname was bestowed on her lifetimes ago, at boarding school, when her fellow inmates discovered she had lived in Saudi Arabia while her father worked for Saudi Aramco, the Arab-American oil company. She had kept the name; she thought it sounded glamorous. But aside from a *burka* boxed up in her attic, that was all she had kept from a time that now seemed as distant as the country she was partially named for.

Today had been a good day. Of course she had to be careful about the good ones. Too many could trick her into thinking she didn't need to take her meds any more. Though no amount of good days would ever make her think that about Gumdrop. Sliding a hand into the canvas bag at her feet, Saudi retrieved an open can of Fancy Feast. An elegant finger filched an extra-large dollop and inserted it between the bars of Gumdrop's cage.

They were coming home two-hundred dollars richer, money won on a greyhound named Daisy Ruckus she'd had her eye on for some time. They could afford to celebrate a bit. This little minute would be just about perfect, were it not for the smell of the man unceremoniously glued to her right thigh. She almost welcomed the fetid aroma of the Salmon Delight Gumdrop was licking with feline delicacy. The triangle-tipped tongue darted in and out, conveying fish flecks into her dainty mouth, while her devilish gold-green eyes were fixed on the gold-headed woman beside the old man.

*   *   *

"Look like *you* the one servin' *her*," Muwanda commented, hoping to shame the cat into looking somewhere else. She'd be glad just to see it blink.

Saudi smiled, gracious as a doily. Taking a tissue from her jacket pocket, she wiped her serving finger, examining and polishing it as if it were a butter knife being set before royalty. Satisfied, she slid the can of cat food into its sandwich bag and zipped the plastic closed with capable fingers. She deposited it in the bag at her feet and looked at her watch.

"No more for you," she told the cat. "Not for another two hours. We'll be home by then. I spoil her, I do," she admitted to Muwanda over the old man's head.

"Say wha-at?" Muwanda leaned forward, trying to stare the cat down. After a moment she commented, "We had us a puppy." That seemed to be the end of it until she remarked like she'd just now remembered it: "That the only reason I stay for the storm. Is that dog. "

Her hands stirred the air. "We runnin' around, I got my kids, my husband, he packin' the car, my sisters, they families, my mother. We like, where we gonna put this puppy?" Her voice hit a treble note. "You understand what I'm sayin'?"

Smitty didn't understand a word of it. An old circus injury had left him deaf in his right ear and the engine at their back was not helping either. He didn't care. He was listening more to the woman's voice than to the news it broadcast. The sound buoyed him, the gliding up-and-back of soprano and bass notes, the clear whooshing murmur of motion in his ears. It was like being up on a swing high in the tent, everything else far away and quiet. He was just a kid when he'd first played on the swings in the Big Top. Till his mother made him come down, for fear he'd break his neck and leave her all alone. He liked the trapeze, liked giving himself to its pendulum force, liked being held by the air as if it was water to float on.

"So we stay." Muwanda's blessed voice lifted Smitty up again. "Me and the puppy. Mm-hm. We stay for the storm. That's right. And we seen things. Things I can't talk about."

Things she couldn't stop thinking about. Bodies floating in the streets. Dead children tied by their shoelaces to the flooded houses they belonged to. People running through the neighborhood wounded, bleeding, fleeing the crack-crack of gunfire and the riot of looting.

"Them other ones," Muwanda concluded, to Smitty's delight. "They go on to my auntie's in Atlanta. But my mother, see, my mother, she don't wanna go. She afraid she not comin' back and she wanna stay in her house, you understand what I'm sayin'?"

Her voice dropped to its lowest register. Smitty sailed down with it on the swing. "And don't you know," Muwanda whispered. "She had a heart attack on the way and she died. Mm-hm. That's the truth. I don't make this shit up."

She sighed hugely. Smitty felt her lung expand against his shoulder. The swing carried him up again with a pleasing hush.

Muwanda put a hand to her cheek. "I didn't get to go to her funeral or nothin'." She shook her head slowly. "It like to broke my heart, mm-hm. Broke sure enough."

"What about the dog?" Smitty asked dreamily, touching down once more. He thought he'd heard her mention something about a dog.

Both women stared at the top of Smitty's head. His waxy yellow hair reminded Saudi of squash. They were surprised to hear him talk at all. He had melted into their sides like a small smelly child, so close to sleep any subject could be discussed and he would not hear it.

"I give it to the lady at the shelter," Muwanda reassured him, as if it were the happy ending to a bedtime story. "She say she gonna take care of it."

She patted Smitty's knee. "Let God and let go. That's all you can do. Right?" Her house was gone, her mother's, too. Before the storm she'd never known such horror. Or such kindness. "The lady give me this sweatshirt."

Raising a hip, Muwanda slipped a cell phone out of her pants pocket and held it up for them to see. "Give me this phone too. Been tryin' to reach my husband, tell him I'm on my way but I can't make it work."

She sat back, patiently punching numbers into the phone with a thumb. Her free hand was slung along the back of the old man's seat. She didn't mind the odor so much anymore. It was something she knew from her before life and in that she could take some strength.

*   *   *

Smitty slumped into the sizeable space left by the absence of Muwanda's arm. His head lolled on her breast.

"Bring it right on in here, baby." The woman drew him in closer like a child, or a puppy. His other hip was braced against Saudi's long thigh. The swing had slowed pleasantly.

Muwanda fingered Smitty's shirt. "What's this you got on?"

Under a faded hospital gown he was wearing a sleeveless t-shirt and trousers too big for him. "I need new shoes," he mumbled.

The two women exchanged looks. Muwanda shook him. "Hey. Mister. How old you be?" She laughed like a tuba might, deep in her chest. "I'm guessin' a hundred if a day."

Smitty grinned into the warm cushion of her bosom. "Ninety," he crackled.

She tapped his knee once. "You made ninety?"

He had impressed her, he could tell. "Or ninety one."

"My mother was fifty-eight when she pass, mm-hm," Muwanda remarked.

"That's younger than me!" Saudi exclaimed, instantly regretting it. From there she proceeded to break another cardinal rule of etiquette by covering one *faux pas* with another.

"Sir?" Her voice came out too loud, too false. "How far you going today, sir?"

The blare of her question interrupted Smitty's sweep up Muwanda's airy notes. He lost his balance, toppling from the swing and falling into the net's taut web. Muwanda's hand came up and tucked him in tighter. Defying gravity, he bounced off the net and grabbed a stationary bar high up in the bones of the tent.

"Lancaster," he mumbled.

"Pennsylvania?" Saudi could hardly contain her surprise.

Smitty rolled his head to stare at her. "Burt."

"Say what-at?" Muwanda was tapping numbers into her phone. She put it to her ear. "Hello?"

"Burt Lancaster?" Saudi echoed Smitty. "Isn't he dead?"

Smitty pointed a finger at himself. "I'm his catcher."

Against her better instincts, Saudi stared at him outright. "Sir, you played baseball?"

The blue mouth curved in a toothless smile. "Datsun Imperial."

Saudi pursed her lips. "Oh, what, is that some kind of car?"

Muwanda spoke into the phone. "Auntie? Hello?"

"Circus," Smitty explained to Saudi, not without effort.

"Wait a minute, wait a minute." Saudi clasped her hands as if beseeching God for clarity. "Did you not just tell me you knew Burt Lancaster?"

Smitty nodded. "I was his catcher."

"His catcher?" Amazement brightened Saudi's face so that for a few seconds it regained some of its former loveliness. She covered her mouth with both hands, excited as a girl. "Yes! Yes! Now I remember! He was a trapeze artist. Before he went into the movies? Yes? I knew that! I don't read *People Magazine* for nothing you know." She sounded quite pleased with herself.

Muwanda snapped the cell phone shut like a castanet. "Who's Burt Lancaster?"

Gumdrop had given up bedeviling her. The cat had turned its back finally and was looking the other way out the window. Its tail flicked from time to time as if it was keeping an eye on her by remote.

Saudi inclined her head toward Muwanda. "You know. The movie star."

"Elmo Gantry," Smitty threw in, to be helpful.

"Elmo?" Muwanda repeated, confused. "That blue one? On TV?"

"Elmer," Saudi corrected Smitty.

\* \* \*

*Elmer. Elmer Gantry.* That's right, Smitty thought. *The Rainmaker. Birdman of Alcatraz.* He had seen Lancaster in the pictures many times. It always gave him a feeling of pride. He didn't know when he'd last laid eyes on old Burt. Time was a con pulled off by clockmakers. His life was a series of stories strung together by time, like underwear on a clothesline. Once he'd been desperate to tell them to anyone who'd listen but now – what were they exactly? He could hardly remember. Surely there had been more than one. In any case, they all started the same way. With his mother.

Smitty's mother had to be thirteen or fourteen when she got sick of life on a farm in Fresno, took baby Smitty by the hand, and walked out of her father's house forever. Mother and son were so close in age, they could have been brother and sister, which indeed they may have been. Her father, Smitty's grandfather – who Smitty secretly suspected was his father, too – never found them, if he ever looked.

The fugitives fell in with a carny, one of those popular traveling girly-shows. His mother was saving up to go to New York City, a place of modern marvels she'd heard tell. Smitty wanted to stay with the carnies so he ran away at thirteen and took up with Datsun Imperial, a circus passing through. At first he was a roustabout, driving stakes, watering animals. But unlike his grandfather/father, Smitty's mother could always find him. It went on like that for years until she finally took her life and that story ended there.

Then there was the next story, a better story, Smitty thought, though it began much the same way. Only in this story his mother is dead and Smitty is grown. He still works the circus. One day he gets promoted to tent rigger in the Big Top. He fools around on the wire sometimes, before they put it up in the air. He's a wiry little Irishman and very limber. He even climbs up on the stationary bars a few times to see what that's like. Then someone gets sick in the act that's working with Lancaster, Lancaster sees Smitty on the bar playing the clown – and the rest is carnival history.

*  *  *

"I met him once," Saudi commented to Smitty.

"Who?" Muwanda was confused. "Elmo?"

"Burt Lancaster." Saudi found herself blushing.

"We had a bar act," Smitty murmured.

"You worked with Burt Lancaster in a bar?" Saudi was becoming exasperated. Really, the old man was pathetic.

Smitty made a crunching noise in the back of his throat. At first Muwanda thought he was choking. Her body tensed. Choking was a problem with old folks; you could crack their ribs doing the Heimlich. It took her a minute to realize the old man was laughing.

"*On* a bar," Smitty corrected Saudi. "No trapeze. Stationary bars. Five of 'em."

He didn't have the breath to say more, though it took no effort at all to recall the thrill he felt every night watching the handsome young circus star making four full-body swings from one bar to the next, shiny and graceful as a dolphin leaping in a tranquil sea of air. Smitty would be perched on the last bar waiting like a regular trapeze catcher, only without the swing. Oh, how he wanted to regale these two gals with the glorious sight of Lancaster flipping down into the net and bouncing back up to catch his feet.

"Wasn't easy," was all he got out.

Lancaster was a lot heavier than he was, not to mention Smitty had his clown costume to wrestle with: a stiff white ruff around his neck, shoes big as flippers with turned-up toes, a mop of curly orange hair, and an oversize red plastic hammer with a cap of gun powder they called a *dummy bullet*.

"That was him. Lancaster. He thought of that," Smitty mused aloud.

"Mm-hm," Muwanda murmured, humoring him.

The orange hair was natural and straight as a pin, so the circus girls permed it to give it some frazzle. The chemicals dyed it pink for years until finally it faded to this Jean Harlow blonde. Back then, the permanent made his hair bounce like corkscrews when Lancaster grabbed his ankles. Smitty would beat the star around the shoulders with the hammer, trying to knock him off his legs. Far below, the crowd booed and shouted with laughter. After a few minutes, Lancaster would climb onto the bar victorious, and Smitty would fall, arms and legs spinning like whirligigs, into the net. The hammer would trigger, the cap went *kaboom!* Smitty would scamper from the tent, holding his rear. Cheers and jeers pushed him out into the night. Inside, high on the bars, Lancaster took his bows alone.

"A whole season we worked like that," Smitty informed the women. Aside from the show when the dummy bullet went off beside his ear, that was maybe the happiest year of his life.

"Present company excerpted of course," he whispered and fell into an exhausted sleep brought on by his clownish antics.

\* \* \*

Saudi was silently debating whether or not to tell her new traveling companions about her own personal encounter with Mr. Burt Lancaster. How strange that she and this derelict old man should share the same famous acquaintance. As a gambler, she knew the odds of that were minuscule. But the real question was: did she really want to squander her good day?

Regret could take the air out of a good day quicker than a hatpin in a falsie. Glamour had once been within her reach, only to evaporate like a dusting of snow in July. Saudi sneered inwardly: it was an embarrassment is what it was. What would she say? That she had once been the poster girl for the Greyhound bus? Where was the glory in that, pray tell?

*  *  *

"Auntie!" Muwanda spoke into her phone in a sudden rush. "It's me, Muwanda. I been tryin' to call you. I'm on my way." She paused, listening, breast heaving. "That's all right, I cry all the time too. Yeah. Yeah. Are my babies there? Ooh, let me speak to them. Auntie? Hello? Hello?"

She popped the phone from her ear and glared at it. "That ain't right," she told it. Her broad face darkened in warning. "They don't call me back, I'm tossin' your sorry electronic ass out this window, mm-hm."

She shut the phone like a clam. Her hand closed over it tightly as if she feared it too could still wash away.

Saudi was picturing the arc of Muwanda's phone exiting the bus, landing in the matted vines that still bore Katrina's footprint. They were passing through a corridor where tornados had touched down. Loblolly pines were broken off like matchsticks snapped by children. Houses were flattened as if by a giant's shoe. On a hillside the grass had been ripped out by the roots. Having wrestled with crabgrass in her lawn for decades, Saudi couldn't help marvel at the storm's cruel efficiency.

It was not much further to Opelika. She would not be sorry to say farewell to her seatmates. She could no more bear their suffering than she could her own; she simply wanted it gone. There was nothing she had not tried on herself, short of electroshock. The only balm she had found was a diabetic old cat she dragged around like a stage prop, and those few ecstatic moments at the track when the dogs were flying and she let herself be Lady Greyhound again.

*Lady Greyhound.* The words conveyed white linen against her skin, fragrant gardenias on her shoulder. For one shimmering New York summer Saudi had been semi-famous. At twenty-four, she was admired and toasted. She had cut ribbons and had her picture taken with other luminaries, like that Jewish conductor Leonard Bernstein, and genuine movie stars, Mr. Burt Lancaster for one.

It was not all glamour. She had to be up and showered before the sun to beat the morning rush-hour traffic. Her make-up was thrown on during the drive from her aunt's house on Long Island to the AA Animal Talent Agency on Manhattan's East Side. The agency was always an adventure. There were show animals of every stripe, donkeys and tigers and ferrets, even tarantulas and rats with union ties and movie contracts. Saudi was there for the silky white greyhound who she then chauffeured across the 59th Street Bridge to the 1964 World's Fair in Queens. Their destination: the Greyhound Bus Pavilion.

Saudi heard herself ask aloud, "Did either of you happen to take in the World's Fair in Queens?"

It was a foolish question she knew. Saudi was fairly certain the woman was too young to have gone anywhere in the sixties. The old man maybe, but who could get a straight answer out of him? Besides, the Greyhound Pavilion sat in an obscure corner of the Travel and Transportation Exhibition across the walkway from the Socony Mobil Oil and General Motors Pavilions. That was where that she and the dog performed. Pretty-faced, strong-limbed, and obedient, it was astonishing how much the dog resembled her escort when they pranced out together onto the exhibition stage.

Muwanda didn't answer Saudi's question. She was busy shaking Smitty. "Hey. Mister. Wake up."

Smitty was not moving. Saudi forgot all about Lady Greyhound and her fleeting fame. The old man was dreadfully still. Where was he going anyway, she wondered, a fellow of his age and means? She was not convinced by his Burt Lancaster story either; it lacked plausible detail.

"Mister!" Muwanda poked Smitty's shoulder. "Where you goin'? Huh?" She raised her voice. "You got a ticket? Let me see your ticket, honey."

Smitty shivered. He was terribly cold. His hands and feet had all but disappeared. "New York," he mumbled.

Saudi gasped. Though she avoided metaphysics on principle, she was overly fond of coincidence, almost to the point of superstition. If she saw the words "Saudi Arabia" in a headline or on TV, that was a sign to buy a lottery ticket. If she passed someone walking a greyhound, it was time to sell some stocks. Coincidence, she was convinced, was life's true pattern, people and events crisscrossing each other like the layers of cane making an interlocking design on the seats of her dining room chairs. Her life was riddled with coincidence. The old man was merely its latest affirmation.

She shed all doubt of him. Their lives were entwined through their mutual friend, Burt Lancaster. Everything had already happened and was just waiting to be revealed. So it came as no surprise to her that the old man was headed for the very place where she had a good day all summer long!

\* \* \*

Muwanda patted Smitty's pants' pockets, looking for a ticket, a VA card, anything. She placed an arm across the front of his body and lifted him up to check his back pockets. She was muscular from years of wheelchair transfers and invalid baths. The man weighed eighty pounds if that, less than one of her nine-year-old twins.

"How'd you get on this bus, Mister?" Muwanda set him down like a broken doll. Things were so confused these days, anybody could slip through the cracks. He could have wandered onto the bus and who was there to notice, or care?

Smitty pressed into the folds of Muwanda's shirt, pursuing her warmth into her body. He was so cold. He had lost his limbs. Only the ride on her voice kept him moving. He needed to keep her talking until his mother arrived.

"You like the circus?" His whisper was muffled by the cloth.

"Mm-hm." Muwanda opened the cell phone again. She did not want to miss a call from Atlanta.

"I didn't ask you mm-hm," Smitty countered breathlessly.

Muwanda chortled. "The circus is all right." She stuffed the phone back in her pocket. Nobody had called her back.

Smitty's face was overtaken by an empty grin. "New York," he repeated.

Saudi marveled. The fine web of happenstance was holding them fast. There was a lesson to be learned here, if only it could be grasped in the next five miles before she and Gumdrop got off in Opelika.

"New York?" Muwanda echoed. "I be likin' this now."

"My – my mother." Smitty struggled to get out the words. It was the start of a new story.

"What about your mama?" Muwanda hovered over him like a cloud on a windless day.

"She's here," Smitty murmured.

"Wish mine was." Muwanda put a hand to her eyes. Her voice scooped up Smitty and held him.

He could see his mother now, way down below the stationary bar he was sitting on. Even in a crowd, his eyes could always find her. She was smiling up at him, waving her cotton candy. The two women were with her too, the soft one and the tense one.

Smitty stood up on the bar. The light swam in his eyes. "Watch this," he whispered and dove.

The air closed around him like an old friend coming home. He sailed and soared, he glided and spun, from bar to bar to bar. The women's heads, gold and silver, grew further and further away.

His mother stood on the last bar. She was waiting for him. He fell into the net and ricocheted up to catch her ankles. Her skin was warm to his touch –

\* \* \*

The phone rang in Muwanda's pocket. "Don't hang up! Don't hang up!" she cried, digging for the phone. "Hello? Hello?"

Her face lit up as if by spotlight. "Oh, hey, baby. How my baby today?" Lifting the arm that supported Smitty, she put a finger in her ear to hear over the engine. The old man sloped gently. His head was practically in her lap.

The bus was pulling into the station. "Opelika!" the driver called out.

Gumdrop meowed once, reliable as an alarm clock. Passengers stood, gathering their belongings, cigarettes stuck between their lips like dowsing sticks guiding them out.

"This is Opelika," the driver repeated. "We will be here five minutes for all my smokers. Keep your eyes open. Don't be late or you'll be lost. Opelika Alabama." The ends of the driver's hands flared like tinted sparks as she released the door and stepped out into the night.

Saudi sat up, startled. Something important had happened and she was certain she had missed it. She rose automatically, holding Gumdrop's carrier in her hand like an extra appendage, and crab-walked past her traveling companions' knees.

"Good luck to you both," she said. She thought that sounded feeble. She didn't even know their names.

The old man did not respond. Muwanda nodded. She was listening intently into her phone. She wagged her fingers at Saudi like she would see her tomorrow. Her hand came down and rested on Smitty's arm.

Reluctantly Saudi started down the aisle. She was certain some opportunity was slipping away. On impulse she reversed herself and came back to stand before Muwanda.

Muwanda put a hand over the phone. She gazed up at Saudi. "Lady? You okay?"

Saudi peered into Muwanda's eyes. They were the color of topaz and very kind, she decided. The woman had lost her house, her mother, her dog, and still she was concerned about Saudi.

Saudi opened her purse and removed two new one-hundred-dollar bills. "Here," she insisted. She thought that sounded brusque. "Take this. Please."

Muwanda blinked. Smitty was light as a bird on her thigh. She whispered into the phone, "Don't go away."

Muwanda could not take her eyes off Saudi's satiny nails or the thin edges of crisp paper between them. "Sure enough?" she murmured. A thousand strangers had gotten her this far. Who was she to refuse another?

She slipped the bills from Saudi's fingers. "You my angel," she told her.

"I doubt that very much." Saudi waddled on her heels, revolving down the aisle. Betting on the dogs was a tawdry habit anyhow. Everyone knew those greyhound racers were horribly abused.

Muwanda peered at the old man. His left arm dangled to the floor. He seemed too comfortable to move, like a man taking a cat nap in front of the TV. Muwanda called to Saudi's back. "Angel?"

Saudi halted. She looked over her shoulder and waited.

Muwanda said, "Tell the bus driver this old man has passed."

Saudi's head bobbed up and down as if she'd received information in a foreign language and was translating in her head. This old man has passed. This old man was dead. He had died while sitting beside her. Their bodies had been touching.

She kept her gaze on Muwanda, refusing to look at Smitty's ash-gray skin, the bruised and sunken lips. How peculiar to meet someone for the first time on the day of their death.

"It wasn't Burt Lancaster," she told Muwanda. "It was that other one. With the radio show. What was his name? Arthur. Arthur Godfrey. That was him."

She had not been a celebrity either. The dog was the real Lady Greyhound, the dog was the star of the show. Saudi got to hold her leash and look good and let men call her Lady Greyhound because they were too lazy or too shy to read her name tag. There were no gardenias, either, though the suit was real linen, even if she did look like a stewardess in it.

But to be present for the death of Burt Lancaster's catcher? How rare a thing was that? A guilty elation infused Saudi, as if she had passed a test she hadn't studied for. She would tell his story wherever she went, even though it meant admitting where and how they had met. There was the coincidence of being in the right place at the wrong time, or the wrong place at the right time, however it served.

Clutching Gumdrop's cage with both hands, she was already rehearsing what she would say to the driver as she went down the aisle.

*   *   *

"You still there?" Muwanda spoke into the phone. "Let me call you back."

Snapping the phone shut, Muwanda eased herself out from under Smitty and sighed. It would be tomorrow now before she saw her kids.

Everything that mattered to her was in Atlanta. It was true they might have a better life there. Her before life was buried in the gulf and maybe that was a mercy but she wanted it back. She wanted her mother back. That life existed nowhere now but in her mind and it was possible she could lose that, too, before she and this old man met up again.

Muwanda turned Smitty's body so that he lay flat on his back. His eyes fell open, staring up. She straightened his arms and legs along the three seats. For a moment, she put a hand to the soft bright hair. Then she dropped her hand over his eyelids and closed them.

"I be glad somebody going home today," she said.

# Acknowledgments

These stories were inspired by Blaze Foley – his music, his memory, his traveling shoes. Glyn Thomas and Yukon Grody were the first champions of the writing. Many good readers – Karen Rosen, Pat Green, Elena Skye, Sas Thomas, Marnie Andrews, Jeff Jacobson, Craig Fuller, Mitchell Smith, Tony Boatright, Bobbe Toub, Thadeus Bradley, Jean Hudson, Margery Bouris, Bill Bouris, Dee Boyle, Erin Boyle, Mia Wood, Mike Thomas, Jill Olesker, June Stein, Mary Davin, Diana Hartel, Katherine Cortez, Amelia Penland Fuller, Jill Silverman Pekar, Kathryn Lichtenberg, Ira Wohl, Anna Stein, Chase Twichell, Kathryn Grody, Sean Thomas Ogle, and Steve Voinche – read all or some of the stories. You offered insight, corrected my geographical confusions, and most importantly, encouraged me to keep going. Chris Manheim cast her meticulous eye over the final draft. Linda Gluck made it look good on the screen. Susan Castner lent her considerable proof-reading talents and Kevin Triplett gave technical and moral support. To all of you, my heartfelt appreciation and love.

I would also like to thank James E. Lewandowski for his book *Road Hunter in the Land Between the Rivers,* which opened up the world of gun truck crews in Iraq, and the Thomas Brothers for an education in cockfighting. Any license I took (pun intended) with routes and schedules was in deference to the demands of fiction.

Lastly this book belongs to the ticket agents, baggage handlers, bus drivers and fellow passengers I encountered over 30,000 miles, the ones who told me their stories and who listened to mine.